OBLIVION'S EDGE

by

Kim Kacoroski

OBLIVION'S EDGE

Cover art illustrations by Kim Kacoroski, Phillipe Velasquez, and Masha Tatarintsev

Visit the author website:
http://kimkacoroski.com

ISBN: 978-1-947036-04-8 (Paperback)

Version 2017.14.03

Book Three of Oblivion Series

Oblivion's Edge III

Other Books in the Oblivion Series

Escape from Oblivion I

Beyond Oblivion II

Oblivion's Deal IV

Flight from Oblivion V

Books in Flight Series

Flight from Oblivion I

Eagles's Flight in the American Revolution II

Flight of the Ascendants in the American Revolution III

Choices from the American Revolution IV

Bridges of Flight before the American Revolution V

Testimony VI

Books in the Camelon Series

The Promise of Camelon I

The Dragons of Camelon II

History of the World According to the Druids III

The Kingdom of the Golden Tara V

Bridges of Flight before the American Revolution VI

INTRODUCTION

*Tune references have been included with this version of **OBLIVION'S EDGE**, which portray range of emotion and delineate boundaries. The effect exposes whatever is hidden in the shadows. Elemental wear and tear of ocean waves smooths the rough edges of rocks. The ups and downs of the story polishes the various relationships, while shining light on the darkness.*

Chapter One

Sometimes it is time to make a stand

For the better

Even if you don't understand

What is going on

Tune Reference: *Stop And Stare*

----OneRepublc

THE SUN BROKE through the clouds, casting a silver light over the waves that led to a single point on the horizon. Joan could make out the figures dancing in the glistening stream across the ocean. They waved and called to her in silent frequencies that warmed her and expanded her world. She knew them as the merpeople, a hybrid between the human form and fish spirit. They always refreshed her and communicated many thoughts on the planet and how it all related to her life. They provided a multidimensional perspective on her affairs that she cherished. Joan yearned to see life in a broader perspective, and the merpeople responded. They cast their perspectives in golden hues rather than silver linings, with an energy as expansive and lighthearted as shimmering waves in the sunlight peeking between gray clouds. She loved their tranquil, light-hearted dance in the waves. Often she saw herself there in the shiny reflections, dancing with them.

When Joan wasn't spending her time in seaport towns off the coast of Maine, she worked as a physician at a hospital in Portland. Whatever she saw in the office that day came with her to the beach. She could always count on synchronicity to pull her through. Joan never carried her work as a burden, instead it became the waters of her reflection that she would bring to the ocean like a river returning to the source. The merpeople would dance with her thoughts and then send them to the silvery skies above. Somehow the interaction leveled her. She recalled the vision of a particular exotic fish in the local aquarium. This particular fish could simultaneously see above water as well as below. She felt like this fish when she entertained the merpeople's perspective. They always seem to connect with the cosmic forces governing life itself. This vision uplifted her for the next day and allowed her to watch the machinations of world affairs underneath a cosmic light.

Today the synchronous message that came from the ocean waves centered on her last visit to the National Mall. She had been there with the lover that she would be meeting this evening. Perplexed over the message concerning the National Mall and Ernst, she slowly recalled the monuments that they had viewed together. Their argument erupted at the FDR Memorial. It had begun brewing shortly before they entered Jefferson Memorial. She could not remembered what their discussion had been about, only the distinct impression that she and Ernst were not meant for each other. His manner had been cynical. The merpeople in the distant light encouraged her to reflect on this subtlety for the evening.

As Joan walked along the water's edge, she spied a sand dollar tossing in the waves moving towards her. A gift from the sea clued her in. Her tide had come in. Not just a shift, now came the time to make a stand.

No more watching and waiting for the arrival of results. Without getting her feet wet, Joan picked up the beached sand dollar and examined it closely. Still alive, the circular disc arrived with a purple velvet cover. Joan glanced at the figures in the distance and thanked them for the message, which resonated with a poem she had written for a Yanni, a friend from college. It was entitled *Lifelines*.

> *I passed the monkey rope*
> *From my ring finger to my neighbor*
> *It wasn't long before Queequeg appeared*
> *He had another sand dollar for me*
> *Fresh currency from the sea*

The time had come to create and maintain life-sustaining relationships. She hurled the living disc back into the water like a frisbee. For a moment Joan felt suspended in endless time, experiencing a sense of grace that someone finds when they open a flower or escape a fatal wound. It was peaceful, like the glowing white sea gull riding the turbulent waves in the distance. Not having gone over the brink, Joan remained steadfast on the edge like a fearless sea captain staring over at a sea of chaos, extrapolating a positive outcome.

With the incorporation of this inner vision, Joan left the beach and headed for her vehicle parked along the road. Driving out of the city, she went home to her lake cottage. She changed clothes and put on something more casual and feminine. After feeding her dog, she drove to a small seaport town on the coast. Intent on her plans to meet Ernst for dinner, she never the noticed the car following behind her. The driver pulled into the parking lot across the street and watched her go into the restaurant.

A young man with carefully groomed short brown hair rose from a table across the dining area. "Hello, Joan," he greeted her with a little kiss on the cheek as he pulled a chair out for her.

"Thank you, Ernst," she smiled, tossing her long auburn hair behind her. She wore a light-colored flowing skirt, organic tee shirt, and sandals. Sitting down opposite his place at the table, Joan pondered whether their relationship remained in sync and sustainable. The message from her afternoon walk near the waves prompted her to examine all her relationships for the presence of synchronicity.

"Would you like a glass of wine?" he asked.

"No thanks. It was a long day at work. I'd better stick to drinking green tea tonight, otherwise I'll be asleep soon." Though Joan slumped back into her chair with a slight air of resignation, she brightly continued, "Let's get some pita bread and hummus as an appetizer. I am so hungry."

Something about the first few seconds of their encounter told her the affair with Ernst was over. They didn't share the same goals. He had brought the residual debate from their trip at the National Mall to the table. Joan had hoped Ernst would drop it, but he still seemed to be looking for a fight. His manner contrasted sharply with the vision of the resting sea gull bouncing over the waves. He didn't seem as warm and as alive as the feel of the soft sand dollar between her fingers.

"I'm gonna order a beer," Ernst informed her.

"Don't let me stop you," Joan responded as she shifted her gaze to the view outside the window. A sailboat motored to dock at the adjacent pier. Her ship had come in. Instead of escaping, Joan stood contentedly on the edge like a sea captain at watch and visualized a positive outcome. Realizing quickly there remained a lot to be said for solitude, Joan returned her attention to the man in front of her and demanded, "What kind of vegetarian dishes do they serve here?"

"I think they have a tofu stir fry and a lentil curry. We can ask the waitress when she returns with our drinks," Ernst, suggested as he folding his arms across his chest. He slumped in his chair with a sideways glance at Joan.

They placed their orders after Joan quizzed the waitress on vegetarian menu options. Within twenty minutes, the woman brought out a hamburger and fries for Ernst and a salad for Joan.

"The red curry soup is on its way," the waitress announced, placing Ernst's dish in front of him. Then she left them alone.

"Heard anything interesting today?" Joan asked Ernst. She knew to ride this one out and let events unfurl like the ocean tide.

Ernst dropped his arms, leaning further back in his chair as he took a long sip from his beer. "Well, the heat wave in the Midwest continues. The Soviets continue to occupy Afghanistan despite the US boycott of the Summer Olympics."

"I wonder whether the Soviets would boycott the Olympics if NATO were the ones bombing Afghanistan?" Joan questioned, though she could already predict Ernst's reaction.

"It is like we are back in the Cold War again," Ernst remarked.

Joan nodded and sipped on her tea as she watched the people scurrying around the sailboat to tie it down in its berth. Though Ernst had not surprised her with his glib response, she pressed him as she observed, "The Soviets must be very competitive. Any news on the hostages in Iran?"

"Nothing has changed, except that it might affect the President's reelection," Ernst surmised.

"Just as long as someone doesn't decide to run a counter operation," Joan speculated, fishing for more information on Ernst's position.

"What do you mean?" Ernst asked.

"You know, the ol' give-'em-arms-for-hostage deals," Joan said. It had dawned on her that Ernst represented a ship passing in the night.

"Like an Iran-Contra operation? Who would do something like that?" Ernst questioned.

"I don't know," she ventured, hoping to salvage something positive from their relationship. "Iran is in a middle of a war with Iraq. This is one way to bring the U.S. back into a Mideast conflict. *War Is a Racket* was written by the most highly decorated general of WWI."

"You just want peace," Ernst decided. "I say go kill a commie for mommie. "Didn't they try to hire the most highly decorated general of WWI to overthrow FDR."

"Yes, General Smedley Butler fingered the military-industrial complex, though I think that the racket succeeded in assassinating FDR with coumarin," Joan surmised, steering the conversation elsewhere before Ernst sunk her.

"You'd be the one to know, doc," Ernst said as he looked down and shook his head. "Go with the winners. It is called progress."

"I don't think that bombing the heck out of country is the way to get our democratic point across. It is not about communism; it is about oil," Joan said as she looked at the waitress, who had just placed her soup on the table.

The waitress quickly bowed her head and left. She obviously did not want to participate in a political discussion between lovers. Although Joan had not said it out loud, the words "man overboard" filled the atmosphere at the table. Sitting back in her chair, she refused to entertain Ernst anymore and distanced herself.

"We need to show the world how strong we are," Ernst insisted. "Make them think twice about seizing hostages."

"Are you signing up for the Gulf War?" Joan asked, wondering whether the man in front of her had a synchronous bone in his body. "Or are you trying to revive the Civil War?"

"What Gulf War?" Ernst questioned her. "They assassinated Lincoln to pave the way for corporate profit. The railroads had a hand in it, you know."

"The Gulf War you are proposing," she answered before accusing Ernst. "Have you been watching too many *M.A.S.H.* reruns lately? You are making a glorious excuse for a crusade against some oil-soaked country in the Mideast. With respect to Mr. Lincoln, the railroad companies are intimately connected with the oil companies, which brings us to the present CIA."

Ernst looked at her and shook his head. "Forget Lincoln. Darwinism rules," he told her. "Survival of the fittest."

"Makes you wonder who funded Darwin. What about diversity as the key to survival?" Joan questioned, losing her appetite. The ensuing turbulence almost made her seasick. "Maybe that works in the fish bowl, but I don't think it applies to all species. Not all animals that are the fittest manage to survive. Look at the wolf, for example, that species relies on group effort for survival. They are too puny to take down a larger animal on their own, so they run in packs."

Ernst held a Doctorate in Oceanography and worked for the state of Maine. Little did he realize that Joan had suddenly started to view him as an overpaid ocean tide monitor. His approach to global currents seemed too simplistic.

"OK, so who do you think is responsible for the terrorist bombing in Bologna?" Ernst quizzed, changing the subject to derail Joan.

"The reports say that a neofascist group claimed responsibility," Joan answered. She noticed Ernst's attempt to throw her off. Steadying herself, she responded, "The papers dubbed the incident as the worst atrocity in Italy since WWII."

"Yes, and the Supreme Court ruled earlier this summer that GMOs could be patented," Ernst added, getting Joan further off track. GMOs referred to genetically modified organisms.

"What are you getting at?" Joan asked with a perplexed expression. Rechecking her orientation, she had a sickening feeling in her gut about the course of the conversation as well as the relationship.

"An electric company created a bacteria that could break down crude oil spills in the ocean," Ernst said. "It's great and now it will be easier to get funding for research."

"Sounds fishy to me," Joan commented, refusing to give an inch. It became time for all hands on deck, and she persisted. "Does the electric company own stock in the oil companies? Next thing you know, the neofascists will be making a profit from the genetically-modified seeds they give to the countries that they bomb."

"Well, the Supreme Court upheld the patent," Ernst continued.

"Look Ernst, I don't think you understand what you are saying," Joan remarked, preparing to sail forward.

"I am considering working for a private company that studies the effect of the bacteria on ocean spills," he announced. "They approached me last week."

"Oh," Joan said, pushing ahead with the wind in her sail. It seemed that the upcoming presidential election polarized the entire nation at a time when the world seemed to be splitting apart. She did not care for any of the options.

"How about coming over tonight?" Ernst asked.

"Ernst, I think that we should talk about the relationship," she accosted him. "Suddenly we seem to be very different people, too different. I once believed opposites attracted each other, but I need more compatibility."

Ernst gazed into the distance and admitted, "I know. I wanted to patch things up a bit."

"I appreciate your effort," Joan replied with a sincere smile. They had been dating off and on since their undergraduate days at the university. Now she felt that they had finally figured the relationship out.

"We'll always be friends," she told him after they had finished dinner. "Maybe it is just that the world has changed since when we were in college."

They rose from the table simultaneously. After exiting the dining room, Ernst walked her to her car and kissed her lightly good-bye. "Call me when you want to hear a second opinion," he laughed as he waved her off.

Joan smiled and released her catch, having pirated something worthwhile from the sinking relationship. She always had appreciated his sense of humor, regardless whether she could follow his train of thought. After backing the vehicle out of the parking lot, Joan turned on the main road and drove home. The car from the lot across the street followed her.

Chapter Two

Those who stalk angels

Are demons

Tune Reference: *One Of These Nights*

----Eagles

JOAN SIGHED DEEPLY with relief when she was almost a half mile away from the restaurant. Satisfied that she managed to get her relationship with Ernst back on track and out of her life, she never noticed the car that followed her in her rearview mirror. Somehow she had taken a fork in the road and focused on what lied ahead. Joan pulled into the long driveway that led to her cottage. Something drew her to the lake this evening. Leaving the car in front of the garage, she walked to the dock and stood at the end. Summer would be over in a month, and already she could sense the shortening days and feel the heavy warmth of the lake in the cooler air.

The lake by the cottage had an inlet to the ocean. It held enough saltwater for the merpeople to frequent. Tonight she could make out the figures of several merpeople in the lake. She greeted them and told them about how she had found that fork in the road and taken a different path from the one with Ernst. Global affairs had finally found their way into her personal life. They told to hold Joan ground and continue to be positive about the future. Leaving the dock with a renewed perspective, she went home to her cottage.

The stalker left his car in front of one of the houses at the end of the driveway and hiked a half mile to Joan's cottage. Peering inside the window near the front door, he was surprised to find the cottage vacant. He was puzzled over her absence. The man walked over to the car parked near the garage and noticed that it was still warm from the drive. After waiting a few moments, he became impatient and went back to his vehicle. In his drug-induced focus, it never occurred to him to check the dock. Opening the door to his luxury car, he got in and drove off. One of Joan's neighbors watched the departure of the man's brown vehicle from his living room window. The driver of the vehicle was tall, dark, and handsome with a sophisticated romantic manner. The neighbor assumed that he was one of Joan's suitors.

After entering her cottage, Joan checked her answering machine for calls. One of her pediatric patients had developed a sudden painful ear infection. Joan returned the call and agreed to make a house call so that the parents wouldn't drive to an emergency clinic two hours away. It would be a long drive with a screaming child. Tossing her medical bag in her sports sedan, she drove to a home fifteen minutes away.

The mother let Joan in the front door and directed her to a small child sobbing on the couch. After inspecting the child's health and obtaining a history, she handed the mother some ear drops and asked her to monitor the fever. Then she applied some light pressure to the child's thorax and cranium. The osteopathic approach had appealed to Joan because it allowed her to use her hands to heal. After some light osteopathic manipulative therapy, Joan obtained better drainage in the child's Eustachian tubes and the pressure inside the ear released. The child was almost asleep by the time she finished.

"Thanks again," the mother said as she brought Joan a cup of herbal tea afterwards. "You have the touch."

Joan softly laughed. It wasn't the first time a person had told her that she was good with her hands. "You're welcome."

"No really, I mean it," the young mother thoughtfully said as Joan left.

The night was still young despite all the events that had transpired since she left work. She drove back home and turned into the drive leading to her cottage. Her neighbor waved her down to stop and talk.

"Are you aware that a swarthy gentleman has been watching your home?" the man asked. Thirty years older her senior, his voice assumed an authoritarian tone.

Joan's face turned pale. She got out her car and stood closer to make sure she had heard him correctly. The man studied her reaction and obtained his answer.

"You have my number. Call me or feel free to call the police if he trespasses. You've met all my friends. By the way, I just ended the relationship with Ernst," she told him. Then she added, "We're still friends, but I don't expect to see him much."

The neighbor nodded. Joan was almost like a daughter to him and his wife. They had known each other for almost eight years now.

"We'll keep our eye out," he promised.

"Thanks," Joan said as she got back into her car. She waved good-bye as she drove off.

Parking her car in front of the garage, she inspected the cottage for signs of an intruder before she unlocked the front door. Everything seemed in order. After she closed all the blinds, curtains, and shades, she dialed the number of an old friend from her undergraduate days at the university.

"Hi Yanni, its me, Joan," she greeted, feeling her heart pounding.

"Hi," Yanni answered. Immediately he sensed her alarm, "How's my nature goddess?"

"There's a stalker at the cottage," Joan told him as she got straight to the point.

"Who do you think it is?" Yanni asked, perplexed by the situation. Besides being a master of caution, Joan was not easily rattled.

"I don't know. It is someone who is dark and handsome," Joan mentioned, though Yanni could tell that she wasn't impressed.

"Do you want me to come over?" Yanni offered as his tone grew serious.

"Yes, could you spend the night?" Joan asked.

"Sure," Yanni replied. "Give me a moment to grab a few things. Tomorrow I'll check the grounds in the daylight."

"Thanks," Joan replied. "I just broke it off with Ernst. I'm on edge and have the shakes."

"See ya in a bit," he told her before hanging up.

Joan brewed herself a cup of chamomile tea and waited for Yanni to arrive. He was like a brother to her. They had known each other since elementary school, though the friendship had not blossomed until college.

When Yanni arrived, he hugged Joan and then went to check the home security system.

"It's working," he told her. "Everything seems in order. Now get some sleep. Do you have to get up for work tomorrow?"

"No, I have this weekend off," she replied as she went down the hall to prepare her bath water. "Now that you are here, I am going to take a lavender soak."

"Sounds good. I am going to set-up in my room. I had a long day developing my pictures in the lab. I'll need to go back to the museum tomorrow to finish the process. Wanna come?"

"Yeah, sure. I feel like just hanging out," Donna said as she drew her bath.

The next day Yanni and Joan inspected the grounds around the cottage. They found some fresh tire tracks near a grove of trees about a hundred yards away from the drive. Yanni kneeled over the tracks.

"Looks like the tracks belong to a new, expensive car. Whoever is stalking you has money," he surmised. "I sense a jilted lover."

"I don't jilt my lovers," Joan insisted. "I just throw them off-track with polite excuses."

"Well, this one can't take a hint," he retorted, rising to his feet. "Let's go check out the merpeople."

Joan sighed and followed alongside Yanni to the dock on the lake. He had taught her how to detect them last summer. Now she found her connection with them indispensable.

"Maybe they have something to add," he said as he stood on the dock and stared into the distance.

Joan noticed a few figures bobbing in the direction of his stare. She relaxed and listened carefully, as if to hear the sound of wind in the trees. Most people learned how to tune-out rather than maintain awareness.

"They have seen him several times," she acknowledged.

"They sense that he has been your Latin lover in the past. They don't like him."

"I don't either, especially if they are referring to Nicholas," observed Joan observed. "Remember Nicholas? He's half-Spanish and from northern France."

"Oh yeah, Nicholas van Buren. He was a flame for the last two years of undergraduate school. You showed me his picture once. The very handsome, young man would have given you anything you wanted."

"That became the issue," Joan replied ruefully. "He would have been able to give me anything I wanted." Then she explained, "I'm just not the wanting type. I told you about the party where I met some of his friends and relatives. They make the movie *Risky Business* look like preschool. It's not my scene. You know me, green tea, tofu, save-the-whales, and women's rights."

Joan turned and faced Yanni, who waved good-bye to the merpeople and thanked them for the information.

"I think we got it now," he commented out loud. "If Nicholas is surrounded with connections such as those, no wonder he is pursuing you. You have become a commodity. He wants you for your Pilgrim bloodlines."

"At the very least," Joan said vehemently. "It will never work. Let's get out of here before he decides to check out the cottage on my day off. I need to regroup," she told him before nodding silently at the merpeople, who were slowly submerging beneath the lake's surface.

"Good. I could use some company in the lab today. Everyone else is on summer vacation. Let's take my car. Keep Nicholas guessing."

They drove away to Yanni's isolated office off the coast. After parking his black sports car in the gravel lot, he and Joan walked onto the pier and went inside the single-story building. As he busied himself with the photos in the dark room, Joan admired the collection of Greek vases that he was cataloging. The circumscribed artwork on each vase told a story.

"Let's see," she began. "The institute is saving the most erotic ones for New England's fine arts museums."

"No, they go to the museums on the West coast owned by the wealthy. People in California are less uptight," he joshed. "You must remember that during the Golden Age, the only one straight in ancient Greece was Pericles himself."

"And they exiled him," Joan retorted. Then she went over to examine the photos that Yanni was hanging up to dry.

"How's Adonis doing on the Crete expedition?" she asked as she peered over his shoulder at the photos of sunken ancient Greek ships.

"Oh he loves it, but writes that he misses me and my sexy body," Yanni quipped with a wink. Adonis was his gay lover.

Joan laughed. "Ah, young love ..."

"You're one to talk. You just pushed off Mr. Opposite and now there's Mr. Stalker."

"Stalker is scary," Joan admitted. "Mr. Opposite proved to be the timely fork in the road. Though some might call it character development, I feel I can truly say that I've looked at *Love from Both Sides Now*."

"Sounds like a song," Yanni teased.

"I can dance too."

"You are hot, honey."

"Stalker thinks so, but his highs are always drug induced," Joan said as she looked away and peered out the window across the ocean. "I'm scared, Yanni. There is more to Nicholas than what I want to know. I feel that I am being pulled into this evil web despite my attempts to free myself. I am a natural woman."

"Enough said," Yanni observed as he finished hanging the last wet photo to dry. "Let's drive up to Bangor for some Chinese food. There's nothing like getting lost in Chinatown to free a woman's soul."

Joan and Yanni drove to the heart of the Chinese district in Bangor. After lunch at one of their favorite restaurants, they walked around the district. Besides being crowded with people from various regions of Asia, the streets were full of small busy shops stacked to the brim with curios and products.

"Look Joan," Yanni pointed as he ushered her into a shop full of Chinese teas and herbs. "Maybe what you need is more ginseng to beat off Nicholas."

"What! And start World War III?" Joan joked as she stepped inside the store to browse through their collection of teas. She selected some jasmine and chrysanthemum tea varieties as Yanni made small talk with the middle-age Chinese American behind the counter.

"What do you have to protect damsels in distress?" Yanni inquired of the gentleman.

Yanni nodded in Joan's direction as the gentleman glanced in her direction. He smiled with shining eyes as he quickly studied her before she could hide behind the tall shelves of green tea. She had overheard Yanni's question. Within a few moments she regained her courage and approached the counter with her purchase.

"Here," the gentleman announced as he produced a small red silk purse for Joan. "Gift for you. It brings good luck."

Curious, Joan glanced at the gentleman's shining eyes before she gently opened the red silk purse. The purse contained a jade grasshopper, which could be worn as an amulet. Joan studied the light-green grasshopper and held it in her palm.

"It is very cute. I like it better than Jiminy Cricket. Thank you so much," Joan told the shopkeeper as she replaced the grasshopper in the silk purse. The shopkeeper watched her stuff the amulet in her jeans and pat the pocket lightly for safe keeping.

"Good luck for you!" the shopkeeper repeated.

Then Joan asked him for some leather poultices for ankle sprains and pills for stomach aches. The gentleman shopkeeper found her remedies and rang up her purchases. Yanni remained quiet for the moment. With broad smiles and happy grins, they waved good-bye to the shopkeeper and walked down the street to Yanni's car.

Once inside, Joan removed the silk purse from her pocket and reexamined the jade grasshopper.

"Do you think it is my totem?" Joan reflected out loud. She felt entranced by the lightheartedness the object inspired in her.

"Yes," Yanni replied as he sped onto the main highway back to the coast. He lightly teased her with the fake accent of a Chinese sage, "Ah, little grasshopper, there are many dance steps to learn."

Joan laughed and shook her head. Then she placed the grasshopper purse back in her pocket. Gazing out at the wide expansiveness of the ocean along the highway, she suggested, "Let's stay at your place tonight."

"I was just thinking the same thing. I want to stop at the health food store first and get a few things for dinner and breakfast."

"Great idea," Joan agreed.

Yanni steered off the highway and parked near a tiny store in one of the coastal towns. Then he went inside the store as Joan read through the advertisements on the bulletin board. Several of them caught her attention. One advertisement announced a *chi gung* class for energy cultivation and development. Another notecard advertised an *akido* class. On a third card, a homeopath advertised her services with an energy worker. After looking over the bulletins, Joan went over to help Yanni carry out his groceries.

"This looks great," she said, reviewing his selections. "I want to call on some of these ads when we get to your place."

They drove to Yanni's apartment overlooking the bay and entered. Yanni dropped off his goods in the kitchen and directed Joan to the room across the hall. Some of her things were still there from her last visit. They frequently spent the night when they visited each other. They were familiar with each other's lives like a close brother and sister. After placing some of her things in the room, Joan made a few phone calls. The homeopathic practitioner could see her in a few hours. She practiced only two miles away in an office close to town.

"I've made an appointment with the homeopath," Joan told Yanni as she helped him finish unpacking his groceries.

He dropped her off at the office near town as he headed back to his lab to check on his photos. Joan opened the door to the clinic and peered inside the reception area, which seemed more relaxed and airy than the offices in the hospital where she worked. She entertained a fleeting notion that she had chosen the wrong profession, but the thought disappeared when she decided that she came here to learn. Joan filled out the detailed information form left waiting in the quiet lobby. Nobody else remained in the room.

After a few minutes, a middle-aged woman entered the reception area and introduced herself.

"Hi, my name is Dr. Englehart. Please come in," she said as she shook Joan's hand and directed her to a soft chair in the next room.

Joan handed her the information forms and settled into the chair. She watched the light from a sunbeam sparkle across the adjacent wall. There was a plant in its path, soaking in the rays. The woman held a Doctorate in Psychology, but practiced as a certified homeopath. Homeopathy included a form of medicine developed during the nineteenth century in Germany. Based on the Law of Similars, homeopathy earned success during several European epidemics.

The homeopath reviewed Joan's information and asked her a series of questions. Then she explained the homeopathic remedy she had chosen for Joan.

"This should help break the connection you have with the stalker," Dr. Englehart said. "There may be more layers. It seems that the stalker is connected to the same opium runners that traded with China and financially supported many of the major ivy-league schools. Recall that the American Revolutionaries also dumped opium as well as tea during the Boston Tea Party. You are enlightened without the use of hallucinogenic drugs. The stalker uses drugs to simulate euphoria and pursues you like an addiction. It must have been quite a spiritual shock to meet his 'family' connections. I suggest that you continue to avoid him wherever possible. Assassins since the time of the crusades used hallucinogenic drugs to create Murder, Incorporated. The drugs split the users from their spirituality, whereas some used drugs in the 1960's to find spirituality. In the homeopathic form, they are used now for spiritual emergencies and integration."

"Then there is Leibniz," Joan recalled.

"Leibniz?"

"He inspired the American and French revolutions only to sell out in the end," she explained, absentmindedly as she recalled her college days with Nicholas. "He played off Newton as the father of calculus."

"It involves an energetic betrayal," the homeopath observed.

"An intellectual betrayal," Joan continued. "My friend Yanni often teased me about getting high off integral calculus. I swirled in the intellectual trauma."

"You may have something there. You're very sensitive, even to innuendo. You'll need support with a Lady's Slipper botanical essence, which will tone your nerves and keep you on track."

"So it is more than just the fork in the road. It is a spiritual crisis," Joan remarked.

"Yes," the homeopath answered.

Chapter Three

Kaleidoscope eyes

Merge the pattern

Of a dissociated world

Tune Reference: *Lucy In The Sky With Diamonds*

----Elton John

AFTER LEAVING THE homeopath's office, Joan waited for the bus at a nearby stop. A car that she recognized from the health food store whizzed by. When she saw the driver, she panicked and hid herself in the bus stop cubicle. The driver was her former lover from college, and the one that she and Yanni had suspected. She feared that Nicholas might circle back and accost her on the street while she stood alone. Fortunately, the bus arrived early and quickly drove off before the car returned. Watching out the windows, Joan continue to monitor the route for any signs of Nicholas. She concluded that he must have missed her.

When bus dropped her off near the secluded apartment complex, Joan hopped out of the bus and ran up the flight of stairs. She unlocked the front door and checked inside for signs of an intruder. After she felt satisfied with the security check, Joan called Yanni at work and told him to watch for Nicholas' vehicle in case he might follow Yanni to his apartment.

"I think the homeopathic remedy threw Nicholas off," Joan observed. "I'm going to lie down for a moment. I'm suddenly feeling very sleepy."

By the time Yanni returned home, Joan had fallen into a deep sleep. He placed an extra blanket on her and went out for a swim workout, leaving a note on the counter for her in case she awoke in his absence. He could be found at the pool inside the apartment complex.

The next day Joan attended the *chi gung* class at the college. There were about sixteen people that showed up for the training. Joan enjoyed learning the new exercises, which reminded her of childhood ballet classes. After class ended she felt much more confident and clear about her present situation. Yanni drove her home later in the afternoon.

"I'm going back to the cottage tonight," she told him during the drive. "Thanks for your help and wonderful friendship. I feel like I'm on track now. The homeopathy and the *chi gung* class seemed to help. Maybe all it took to break the energetic connection was a little jade grasshopper."

Yanni smiled. "You seem much better now. Call if you need anything. The merpeople will keep an eye on the place for you."

"Maybe I should connect with the leprechauns on this issue," Joan proposed quietly. "Connecting with those close to the earth spirits might offer other kinds of information on the stalker or Nicholas."

Yanni glanced at her out of the corner of his eye before he chuckled lightly.

"Well, it's my property. I can do whatever I want, even if it means creating communication interfaces with interdimensional beings," she added with a grin.

Yanni laughed louder. Joan seemed pleased with herself and began laughing with Yanni. He turned into her drive and parked in front of her cottage.

"I'll go retrieve my things while you check-in with the Leprechauns," Yanni said.

"I also need to water my garden. Meet me there," she requested.

"The leprechauns say that he has been backing his car into the driveway and peering through windows. They don't like him either. I gave them permission to trip him up next time. My neighbor and I can have him arrested."

"That's the Joan, I know." Yanni smiled. "Are you sure that you weren't a warrior in your past life?"

"Probably, I'm so peaceable these days," she said flippantly. "My parents must have known when they named me. Though I never would have supported the Dauphin as the King of France in those times."

Yanni and Joan continued laughing until she waved him off and he drove out of the driveway with a wide grin. She returned to work the next day and began inquiring about the stalker with the hospital staff. Several coworkers recalled seeing someone that fitted Nicholas's description. He was either lurking in the halls or parked in the corner of the parking lot. Joan notified hospital security and gave them a description of the stalker. They suggested she park closer to the police station and use hospital security to escort her to her car.

A few days later, Joan made a house-call to the home of a local herbalist, who had come down with pneumonia.

"What's going on with you?" Joan questioned the herbalist after listening to the woman's lungs. "Why didn't your herbal concoctions work for you this time?"

In between hacking coughs, the herbalist explained, "Last week my mother died unexpectedly and a friend lost her baby. I made the mistake of spreading myself too thin, not allowing time enough to grieve. Also I fell-off the boat as we were sailing off the coast yesterday. That ocean water is cold."

"What threw you off?" Joan asked. "You are usually sure-footed."

"We saw something shimmering in the sky and I panicked," the patient answered.

"What?" Joan questioned. She finished examining the woman and sat back to ponder her answer.

"People in these parts are spiritual," she told Joan.

"I know," Joan said with a slight sigh.

"You've got a stalker," the woman said between coughs.

"How do you know?" Joan quizzed. "Does it have to do with your accident at sea?"

"I read energy and I can see his darkness in your field. The cord between you and him was recently broken, but he is still present. He is dark and very handsome. A yellow diamond now links you to him and all the others."

"The others?" Joan echoed.

"Yes, all his dark connections have tentacles encircling you like an octopus."

Joan shuddered. Something about the woman's story resonated with some truth within her. She shook her head and then focused on finishing her work with her patient.

"OK, whatever. Stay on antibiotics until we figure out the rest," Joan instructed, as she regained her sense of humor. "Otherwise, you'll need to be hospitalized. No more evening dips in the ocean. I don't care how many extraterrestrials push you in. Stay warm and process the grief with plenty of rest."

The herbalist smiled and nodded before lapsing into a coughing spasm. Joan watched the herbalist struggle with whatever triggered the cough. She decided to keep it simple.

"I'll be back for the rest of the story and maybe you can help me throw the stalker out of my auric field," Joan suggested with a light sense of humor. "Meanwhile I am going to consult with my friend who taught me how to connect to the mermaids in my lake, not to mention the leprechauns around my home."

"I know," the woman said quietly. "They told me. We are all in a big fix these days. Did I ever tell you that my grandmother used to levitate her wood stove for practice?"

"Later," Joan insisted. "I believe it, but you need to get some rest now."

Joan took a deep breath and headed out the front door to her parked vehicle. She looked around before she got in the car. All the nature spirits seemed quiet. The environment felt eerie and a chill ran up her spine. She ducked inside the car, locked the doors, and turned on the heat. Then she drove home.

Joan returned to the herbalist's home two days later to check on her. The woman had made a remarkable recovery and showed Joan some of the botanicals that she had used. They walked together around the garden while her children played nearby.

"Here," the herbalist pointed as she pulled a bottle of St. John's Wort oil from her pocket. "You'll need this for protection from the stalker. Massage this oil into your skin so that you can't be tracked. The Native Americans used the oil for the same purposes. I use it in domestic violence cases. It throws off stalkers."

Joan thanked her and paid for the oil. As she was leaving, she asked, "Now can you tell me what caused you to lose your footing on the sailboat?"

"I was protecting a starship in another dimension," she answered.

"Why?" Joan questioned.

"Well, it has to do with the tentacles of the Octopus. You know more about them than you care to admit right now, which is why you haven't completely disengaged from their energetic presence."

"It is a spiritual emergency," Joan commented.

"Yes, it is. The celestials have come to help," the herbalist added. "Some people navigate forks in the road while others take a plunge. For me, it was a plunge beneath the present surface of superficiality, another wake-up call."

Joan smiled and nodded at her patient. "Time for me to go before I hit information overload. I sense there is some synchronicity here, but I need to wait for events to play themselves out."

"Sounds good. I still need time to recover from my experience. We'll talk again later," the herbalist told Joan.

Joan left the home of the herbalist and drove back to the cottage where she relaxed with a few exercises from class. One particular set that she had learned in class helped her communicate better in the other dimensions. Practicing daily, Joan eagerly looked forward to her weekend classes. The exercise sets not only helped her focus her energies for her patients, but she enjoyed the clarity that the exercises offered. After a month, she noticed an attraction for her instructor, Dr. Lawrence McClendon, who everyone called Larry.

Compared to Ernst, Larry seemed refreshing and seemed more compatible with her perception and views on life. He preferred meditating to fighting. Instead of opting for domination over others, he sought self-mastery. She could feel herself being pulled by the vortex of his warm energy and she found it comfortable. It was perfectly natural for students to be interested in their teachers, Joan told herself. This maintained their interest in the class. She sensed that the rest of her classmates loved Larry too. He was a geophysics researcher from Woodsport, Massachusetts. For reasons unknown to his students, he had taken a two-month sabbatical. His friends in Maine knew he had come north to search for his roots and get back-in-touch with his natural spirituality.

Almost six weeks into the class, the old boyfriend from college joined Joan's class. He cornered her in the training hall when she entered. He was dark and extremely handsome with a medium build and French accent, though he carried himself in the manner of a Spanish conquistador intent on exploration and colonization.

"Hi, my love," he greeted Joan.

"Hi, Nicholas," Joan replied. "What brings you to this class?"

"I miss you," he said.

"You haven't called or written for over five years," Joan told him. "I thought we had parted ways."

"I went on a vacation in Maine and decided to look you up," he offered. "My parents send their love. Remember the canary diamond I gave you? It had been my great-grandmother's."

"Oh, I had kept it as a gift, rather than as a token of a committed relationship."

"I want you, Joan. I want us to be together," he told her in a hushed, forceful but almost irresistible French accent. He was accustomed to getting his way.

This time Joan backed away as her face paled. She no longer found his manner sexually appealing. The homeopathic cleared the veil of illusion from her eyes and she clearly recognized him as her stalker. Finally, Nicholas's true motives had been exposed.

Then he whispered. "My family chose you years ago. We love you. You are clairvoyant, clairaudient, and a sentient. You can decipher messages from other beings. Come with me now and I will give you the world."

Joan heard his words but remained frozen in fear; any fool could tell that the world had already gone over the edge, perhaps taking Nicholas and company with it. The planet needed restoration rather than possession. She wondered what drugs he had done this morning. She closed her eyes briefly and tried to find a way to escape from this nightmare.

Larry, who had been watching the encounter from the other side of the room, felt moved by the woman's reaction and wanted to help her. He had seen through Nicholas' motives once he walked into class. His training heightened his sensitivity, particularly regarding personal space and boundaries.

"I am asking you to leave this class," he demanded, facing Nicholas squarely in the eye.

Nicholas looked insulted and shook his head at the instructor. Larry maintained his position. A few moments later, Nicholas turned and left the room in a huff. Occurring to him that he was out of line, Nicholas seemed confused suddenly.

Then Larry turned towards Joan, who felt herself falling for the man staring at her with warm brown eyes.

"Are you OK?" he asked her. He wasn't sure what had caused him to intervene in someone else's personal affairs. All of his senses had been aroused by the threat to this woman in front of him.

Joan broke temporarily from the bond that held them together and stepped back. Nicholas was gone and this man's energy had taken his place. Amazed at how this had happened, she curiously glanced up at Larry.

"Yes, though I am still shaking. Thank you for your help. He has been pursuing me for the past several months. For various reasons, he decided to make his move here."

"Go get a cup of oolong tea and we'll resume in a few minutes," he told her.

Chapter Four

The sensuality of the world

Reminds us of our passions

Tune Reference: *It's All Coming Back To Me Now*

----Celine Dion

SIPPING HER TEA, Joan and returned to class holding the warm cup in her hands. The exercises and meditation soothed her frayed nerves. After class she gathered her things and slowly walked towards the exit. She was still dazed from her experience with Nicholas. Everyone else had hurried out of the class and went on their way.

"Thanks again for the intervention," Joan told him as she headed out the door. She was the only student left in the room.

Larry took a deep breath and listened to the voice that came from deep inside himself. He hated the thought of socializing with students, but experience and training had encouraged him to trust his intuition.

"Would you like to go out for a cup of green tea?" he asked. "I know a good sushi restaurant around the corner."

Joan cocked her head to one side as if to be listening intently to a hidden message in the ambiance around them.

"Yes, I'd love to," she said after a few seconds of hesitation.

He quickly donned his jacket and turned off the lights to the classroom. Then lightly touching her elbow, he warmly accompanied her out the door and down the street. Once outside the building, he shifted gears and became Larry the beau instead of Larry the teacher.

Joan had not been so close to his body. She could smell his aftershave lotion on his mustached face and feel the heat rising from his forearms. He escorted her inside the intimate atmosphere of the sushi restaurant. The waiter recognized the instructor and placed the couple in a semiprivate booth. They sat across from each other and ordered a pot of jasmine tea.

"So what's a geophysical teacher like you doing in a place like Maine?" she questioned him as she poured a cup of tea for Larry. Still shaking from the confrontation with Nicholas, she continued to operate in crisis mode and got straight to the point.

Larry cocked his head to one side, listening carefully to the subtleties in her words. He grinned slightly when he felt that he had heard her correctly. Joan had admitted her attraction for him in only a phrase. Sensing safe terrain, he decided to confide in her. Something about her soothed and encouraged him at the same time.

"I'm on sabbatical to get back my connection with nature," he admitted. "I've been working too hard in the rock lab. I am trying to find my roots."

Joan softly laughed. "Let's see, you've found that proverbial fork in the road or took that plunge below superficial reality? Or maybe its a spiritual crisis."

"Yes, it's all of that," he agreed. Convinced that it was his turn to ask a probing question, Larry started, "So what is a student doing being pursued by a jilted lover?"

"I didn't jilt him. I purposely let the relationship fade. He has a Latin temperament, apparently," Joan replied with a slight blush. "I've become his obsession. I think his entire family has become obsessed with me."

"That's putting it mildly," he commented, leaning closer to Joan over her cup of tea.

"I'm very physical," Joan explained nonchalantly. "It's a hazard of the profession. I work as an osteopathic physician at the hospital. I love the human form like an artist. I'm into bodies, either dead or alive."

"I want to know more." He moved closer and looked at her straight in the eye.

"No regrets over the relationship," she confessed with a toss of her right shoulder. He seduced me along the physical aspect of life and he was good at it. I learned a lot about myself and the physical body. Now he wants me for the spirituality that he lacks. You can see why I've taken up martial arts."

"I understand." Larry nodded as he sat back in his chair and sized her up. Then he bowed his head close to Joan again and whispered, "I admit that geophysicists adore the earthy aspects of life, too. We take physical geology and bring it to the metaphysical level. We are more spiritual than we care to admit." Then he added with a fake air of resignation, "It's a tough life."

"People are pretty spiritual in these parts," Joan echoed. She returned his playful joust and succulently placed a piece of sushi in her mouth. Her stare into his eyes grew heavy.

"Yes, I am beginning to see that," he replied softly, allowing himself to be mesmerized by the subtle display of sensuality.

Joan found herself plunging into this current of energy pulling them closer and closer. She knew how to read body-talk quickly and decisively.

She knew the edge between life and death. Automatically, she chose life and refilled Larry's up of tea with another hint of eroticism.

"How about some sake?" Larry urged in a low voice. He smiled and began studying the dinner menu in mock attention. "I am suddenly feeling very hungry. It must be all that *energy* we moved this afternoon."

Joan chuckled slightly at Larry's words. Finding the man across from her sexually attractive, she realized that she had suddenly she emerged from being a student to being a lover. This teacher of hers was encouraging her journey as a human being. Having sufficient life experience, she had mastered the basic exercises quickly and added her own individual interpretation. Joan moved into the next level with grace and ease. Sensing her release from her cocoon like a butterfly with new wings, she realized that her teacher had slid from behind his social mask and had become her knight.

"Yes, I'll have a glass of sake," she responded in a slight daze, briefly recalling the homeopathic that she had taken over a month ago. She could not have imagined the rapid development of this romance. Everything must have shifted with the little jade grasshopper that the shopkeeper had given her in Chinatown. Yet, she warmed with the sense of a path familiar to her soul.

Now that casual formalities were out of the way, they grew serious and ordered dinner with the sake. They seemed to be on the same wavelength, pursuing the same goal as the dinner grew more sensual by candlelight. The sake continued to lighten their spirits and placed them on a higher level of reality than what they had ever known in this lifetime. By the time the food arrived, they were lightly kissing between bites. Having trained together for almost two months, they communicated with their bodies and few words were spoken for the rest of the evening. They allowed themselves to be carried by the swiftness of events and understood that the moment had come to put one's oar in. It was almost as if they could sense each other's thoughts, but it was more than just a mental connection. They could enjoy communicating with all their senses and harmonize with the direction it took them like two dancers in a chorus line.

They indulged in the swirling sensation of each other's energy and it filled them. Being astutely aware of the uniqueness of the present experience, they both yearned to take it to its fullest potential. It was as if they had been practicing for this moment all their lives. After dinner they walked a half of a mile to an inn, which afforded an expansive view of the Maine coast. They checked into a room and continued kissing. For a brief eternity, they gazed outside the window at the sea view. An ocean breeze from the opened window drew their bodies closer together until they found the warmth of each other's breath. They turned and began lightly kissing each other as they became locked inside their own little world. Removing Joan's pants, he ran his hands up her thigh and carried her away to a chair hidden on the other side of the window's curtain. Falling against his chest, she heaved long breaths with every caress. He removed his shirt and delved into the moist crevices of her body. Gently he ran his hands underneath her shirt and removed the rest of her clothes. Joan voluptuously kissed his moist lips as he removed his pants and felt her slide into him. A sudden rush left them temporarily senseless before they renewed their fervor with the calm confidence of professional talent. Both knew what they wanted. Together they steadily produced results without pausing for rest.

During some point in their silent conversation, Joan verbalized the obvious, "I need to leave early in the evening. I have work tomorrow morning."

Larry responded with a lingering wet kiss on her right ear. "No worries," he assured her. The rhythm of their heated embrace quickened and he carried Joan to the bed where her lover took the plunge, sending them both to the heights of rapture for several hours. After resting lightly, they showered together while kissing warmly under the spray. They didn't want the day to end.

When they finally checked out of the room, he quietly walked her down the street to her car. Larry gave her a soft kiss on the cheek before she drove off.

"Thank you for being my knight," she told him as she planted a subtle moist kiss on his upper lip. "I'll see you at class next week."

They waved as she drove off. Joan drove down the two-lane highway to her cottage by the lake. The winding road took her through beautiful forested hills and valleys. She turned down the long drive and noticed several police cars parked by her neighbors' house. In the darkness the lights of the police cars shone brilliantly around the driveway. Joan parked her car along the side of the narrow road and got out to see what had happened. Her neighbors and the police had been waiting for her.

"Oh good, there you are!" her neighbor greeted. The police standing around his wife smiled slightly and nodded. "We had your stalker arrested."

One of the officers showed her a picture and asked Joan to identify the man. She gasped when she recognized him. Her head began to spin and she felt a little faint.

"That's Nicholas van Buren," she told them after she took a deep breath.

"Are you pressing charges?" the officer questioned Joan.

"Yes," she replied.

"OK. I'll fill out the report. We'll be in touch," the officer said as he handed her some legal copies.

"Thanks," Joan said to her neighbors and the police. "I feel more secure now that he has been caught."

"He has been jailed on drug charges. We found some stashed in his vehicle," the other officer added before they exited the neighbors' living room.

Joan sighed with relief and then excused herself. "I'm going home to relax now. It has been quite an ordeal. Thank you so much for your help."

When she arrived home, she left messages on both Yanni's and Larry's phone that Nicholas had been arrested for trespassing and possession of drugs. Then she went to bed and tried to get Nicholas out of her head. As her head hit the pillow, she heard her phone ring. She let her message machine screen the call. When she realized the caller was Yanni, she answered.

"Hi," she said. "I was just getting ready for sleep."

"I had to call when I heard that Nicholas was stalking you," Yanni told her. "I'm so glad they caught him. I always thought that he was from a different planet."

"Yes, I know. He's from Sirius, the dog star." Joan sighed. She had rehearsed these explanations in her head many times. "The one that the Egyptian pyramids point to. He's a Serpentine."

"When did you figure this out?" Yanni asked in a soft voice. He and Joan had discussed the galactic wars of ancient Egypt many times in college. "You mean the snake that the pharaohs wore on their headdress?"

"They turned everything into a phallic symbol, their beards, themselves---the one female pharaoh had to wear a beard just to fit in."

"OK, so some Egyptians were fixated on genitalia," Yanni said, glancing at Joan and waiting impatiently for further elaboration.

"There is more to a man than just his penis," Joan replied.

"Yes, the rest of us know and enjoy that aspect," Yanni answered. His forehead furrowed as he tracked Joan's train of thoughts. "Have you been working too hard? Getting lost in too many compartmentalized body parts?"

"Probably," Joan admitted. "But, it's the violence that gets me. You know, the other distortions like rapes, murders, diseases...I see it almost equally in both genders at some level or another." Taking a deep breath, she hesitated before quietly changing the subject. "I lost my virginity to Nicholas."

"You never told me this," Yanni acknowledged. "I heard that he was good. I didn't know he was great."

"You were too busy trying to lose yours and then some," Joan retorted. "He was so smooth that I barely noticed. That's what is so scary. You don't want to make a mistake with the first. It sets the stage for the encounters that follow."

"True, true," Yanni wistfully said, gazing into the distance as he briefly recalled his own experiences. "But it all depends on your perspective. Some of us could not lose it fast enough, while others take their time." After a pause, he responded to Joan's concerns, "Look, maybe you needed to wrestle with a Serpentine before you went on to major in disengaged body parts."

Joan quieted. Sometimes Yanni seemed to understand her more than she did herself. She appreciated his perspective.

"Think about it," he continued. "For many years American medicine was symbolized by the caduceus. When the Americans figured out their mistake, they went back to the Rod of Asclepius. So they went from a symbol incorporating two snakes with wings to a symbol with only one snake. If you ask me, a snake is a snake. Snakes are cold-blooded and guided by their instincts."

"We all have reptilian brains. Babies rely on their instincts for survival."

"OK, so you got started with Nicholas," Yanni observed.

"I am concerned about the attraction," Joan revealed. "It could result in a fatality, mine."

"Were you around when they arrested him?" Yanni pursued, pressing Joan for more information.

Joan took a deep breath before beginning her explanation, "No, I had class."

"Oh."

Joan stared at him. With a hint of reluctance, she offered, "I went out with the instructor afterwards."

"Oh," Yanni softly repeated, waiting to hear more of the story. Cocking one ear toward her, he indicated his need for Joan to provide more details.

"He threw Nicholas out," she confided.

"He saved you," Yanni surmised after he remotely viewed the scene.

"Yes, he saved me," Joan softly replied. Now she had lapsed in a more reflective mood. A few hot tears escaped her eyes and rolled down her cheeks. Looking at the ground, she acknowledged the her difficulty with the day's events. "I slept with him afterwards."

"Of course," Yanni told her gently. He understood the gravity of the circumstances. "You are very physical. Some people would deem you a kinesthetic learner."

"It just seemed natural," Joan confided.

"Yes, these things do," Yanni. "Natural is better than supernatural, and more engaging than relying solely on the instincts. You gave up trying to control life and death, which is a good thing for a physician every now and then. You were vulnerable and allowed him into your life."

"He seemed to fit."

"If the shoe fits, wear it," Yanni advised. "Remember to choose your symbols carefully so that you are not manipulated by them. The world exists in a war between good and evil. I think that you realize this now."

Chapter Five

There is a difference
Between angel stalking
And valuing the loves
That keep you alive

Tune Reference: *What About Now?*
----Daughtery

JOAN MET YANNI at the beach after work the next day.

He gave her a warm hug and kiss while retaining a light grip on her elbow.

"You are shaking, my dear," he observed as he stared out to sea. He knew how to give her psychic space. Joan's face was whiter than pale.

"It still frightens me for reasons that I have yet to understand," she admitted as she relaxed with Yanni's hold on her.

"You were right about Nicholas," he whispered.

"It became difficult to see it play out. What a reality check!" she observed as she joined his gaze out at sea. "I had dissociated myself from the possibility. I've seen dissociative states in my trauma patients. They run like a dime a dozen. I find that it is only the psychologists who make a big deal out of the issue. Now I can tell that I've been in one. The homeopathic remedy helped me integrate what my psyche has chosen to suppress. It's all coming back to me."

Yanni put his arm around Joan in a gentle hug. "So tell me more about your knight."

"He directs a Geophysics lab in Woodsport," she told him. "He's sincere, bright, sexy, handsome, spiritual---we seem to share the same outlook on life like two peas in the same pod."

"Well, that's encouraging. Any plans for the future?"

"He returns to Woodsport in two weeks, but he'll continue to teach the class on weekends until the beginning of next summer."

"I'm talking about the personal relationship." Yanni smiled.

"I don't know. I feel like I've known him before in many ways. The relationship comes so easily that I don't find myself thinking about the future. That is what happens when you meet on a deep spiritual basis," Joan commented as she began walking along the beach. Looking down at the sand for a moment's reflection, she added, "You know, it is sorta interesting. I don't feel like pushing anything, like it will all happen on geologic or synchronous time."

Yanni walked with her and begin fishing for shells and colored glass in the gravelly sand. "There's no rush," he said. "But, you have fallen in love."

"I know," she replied. "And I am happy."

The next weekend Joan met Larry in class. Somehow he managed to draw her aside in a private hall. He spoke to her out of earshot from the group, "I'm sorry I didn't return your call. One of my backpacking buddies made it to the emergency room with a broken arm. I didn't get your message until this morning. Can I meet you after class?"

"Even if you had called, I don't think you would have gotten a hold of me. A colleague went on vacation and I've been pulling double shifts. By the time I get home, it is too late to talk." Joan smiled with a slight toss of her head. She studied the man's face before deciding to accept his offer. Then she gauged the reality of the events that had kept them from connecting until now. She wondered why their timing had been so far off during the week. There was something more to learn and she became curious.

"How about some place more private?" she asked, shifting the circumstances of their interaction. She quietly quieted for his response.

"There is a secluded cafe along the highway two miles south. We can meet there."

Although unsure of the commitment, Joan found herself drifting towards him in a similar current that had drawn her to him earlier. She waved her hands and headed back to the training hall after saying, "Yes, I'll met you there later."

Joan began stretching to warm up. None of her classmates seemed to be aware of the burgeoning romance between her and the instructor. She saw Larry josh with several students as they arrived. She felt relieved and secure that the private world they shared had its own special place in the universe. For the moment, he belonged to her, though she hid her feeling with an easygoing air. Joan could tell by the way he looked at her that she had him hooked, noticing the way his eyes hungered with every sinewy flex of her muscle. When the group began training, they harmonized their movements like the inner workings of a clock. Each individual had their own dynamics meshing within the mechanism of the whole. Larry watched her leave the class afterwards as if the romantic interplay of the previous week had never occurred. His eyes misted after she left, but those who lingered never noticed. He gracefully cut the remaining students short and locked-up the training hall when it emptied.

Drawn to her by feelings and emotions that rose from depths that he had never experienced previously in this lifetime, he quickly got into his off-road vehicle. More than anything in the world, Larry wanted her. He wanted to feel her breath ripple over his skin, while holding her close enough to hear her silent whispers and call him. Confidant that he would soon have her, Larry parked his car beside hers and sat beside Joan at a table near the window.

"I love you," he softly said with a soft nuzzle beside her left ear. Captivated by her sweet essence, he delicately left a lingering drop of warm moisture on her skin. Then he pulled away and stared directly into her eyes. Promising to delve into the untouched recesses of Joan's very being, he held her in his spell until she almost collapse.

Joan melted and bowed her head slightly as her arm gently reached for his. Blinking, she noted the fast-moving relationship and determined to steer her craft like she was paddling in white water. "Shall we leave and go to your place?" she ventured, staring away across the room.

"My cabin is just a bit up the road. Follow me in your car," he quietly suggested.

Leaving the cafe almost as soon as they arrived, they waved off the waitress and headed for their cars. Joan drove behind his jeep as he made his way along the highway and turned down some winding roads. She was familiar with the area and drove at a tight clip behind him. Finally stopping in front of a secluded cabin in the woods, he parked and directed her car beside his.

"Cute place!" Joan told him as she bounced out of the driver's seat.

"The fairies and leprechauns think so, too." He laughed, surveying the magic of his surroundings.

"Oh, I can imagine," Joan replied cautiously, unsure whether she had heard him correctly.

Larry went over to her car and helped her with her things. She always carried an overnight bag in the event she had a patient with an emergency. He put his arm around her and their lips met before they made it to the front porch. In a flurry of excitement, their arms reached for new terrain in the relationship. Once inside the cabin, Larry dropped the overnight bag on the table and they picked up where they had left off in the seaside inn.

This time Joan spent the night and left early in the morning. She felt comfortable with the rapid transitions of the romance and began to create space for it in her life.

"Come with me to the cape when I leave next week. Stay the weekend," Larry said as he leaned over her car door to kiss Joan good-bye.

"Let's talk about it during dinner on Wednesday. I'll meet you at the organic restaurant on the Portland wharf. Did we agree on seven?" Joan questioned, returning his kiss before she drove off.

Rearranging her schedule so that she could spend more time with Larry on the following week, Joan took a quick flight to Boston. Larry picked her up at the airport and together they drove to his home along the Massachusetts coast, fifteen miles north of Plymouth.

"How was work?" Joan asked as they neared his home.

"I'm interviewing graduates for a position in the Geophysics lab. I think I found one I want to hire. She has been going to school in Texas and comes highly recommended by a friend of a friend. Whoever accepts the position will start at the end of January."

"Are you going to suggest that she take up martial arts?" Joan teased lightly.

Larry grinned as he admitted, "Well, yes."

He turned in the driveway of his beach bungalow and led Joan inside his small home. She gasped at the breathtaking view of the cape as she entered the main living area.

"What do you do when you are not conversing with fairies and leprechauns?"

"Check in with the mermaids," he answered flippantly while he focused on making Joan feel at home. "Let's go for a walk on the beach when you've settled."

Joan took his hand as he led her barefoot down a sandy path to the edge of the water. They watched the seagulls dive in the surf and squinted at the silver rays of the sun touching the ocean in front of them. Joan did not see any merpeople on the horizon.

"They like to come out at dusk," Larry mentioned, sensing her thoughts.

"Who likes to come out at dusk?" Joan quizzed, acutely aware that she was no longer in Maine with her spiritual acquaintances.

"The sea people that you are looking for," he said as he playfully drew in the wet sand and looked for some of his favorite rocks along the shore.

"How did you know that Yanni had taught me how to find the Merpeople?" Joan teased, knowing that Larry respected Yanni's work in nautical archeology.

"I can sense the wavelength of your thoughts and their direction. One of the hazards of being a geophysicist," Larry said thoughtfully. He knew that Yanni was like a brother to Joan, who cherished the childlike way he viewed the world. "The training just refines the talent. Every teacher knows when their student is doing the alchemy correctly."

"Oh," Joan replied as she absentmindedly began to collect pieces of sea glass.

"Whatever happened to your stalker?" Larry asked.

"Some wealthy politician got him off," Joan responded. "I'm having security alarms installed this weekend while I'm gone."

"Do you think this is the last you'll hear from him?" Larry questioned.

"Yes and no," Joan replied. "The more I heal, the less likely he will pursue me. Now I am finally beginning to understand the phrase *physician heal thyself.* It is an intriguing concept when applied to this situation. It is like being in a house of mirrors and searching for the image that is truly your own reflection."

Larry found a stone that captivated him and held it in his hand as he nodded to Joan's words. He enjoyed listening to her because she had so much depth. Joan stopped and looked at Larry. She noticed that he was listening intently to her.

"I sense that there is more to this than just healing," she confessed. "It is like we are in a spiritual war. I need to do more research on this complex web that once threatened to engulf me."

Chapter Six

Magic is a game

Played by children at heart

Not afraid of finding secrets

Tune Reference: *Games Of Magic*

----Bread

JOAN CONTINUED THE love affair with Larry while pursuing her training. None of her classmates suspected the romantic involvement. She met Larry every other weekend and occasionally he returned to Maine to teach seminars. Meanwhile she kept up with Yanni and his adventures.

"What did you want to show me?" she asked him. She peered at the photos hanging in the room to dry.

"These," he said, handing her some photos from a file.

"Are these from your Mediterranean trip last summer? Joan asked. She saw what looked like a submerged city with three islands connected by underwater tubes. Taking a deep breath, Joan energetically connected with the scene and observed ribbons of light emanating from an area in the middle of the photo.

"So you found the lost city of Atlantis?" she questioned Yanni.

"No," he corrected her while he finished the final touches on another project.

"You are looking at the spirit of the earth," he told her. "It has nothing to do with the structures built around the islands, which, of course, are unmapped. These military-industrial thieves don't know what they are pirating. They only know that it has properties of superconductivity similar to ormus materials. It isn't an ormus material though. There's more to it than that."

"I'm surprised the pirates didn't kill you for these photos," Joan commented.

"They tried," Yanni admitted, looking up from his project briefly to take a deep breath. "But, I found the bomb they planted on the Institute's small jet."

Joan closed her eyes. She wasn't sure she was ready to handle this information. Feeling angry that Yanni had withheld this from her, she calmed herself before letting her temper ruin their friendship.

"I started seeing your homeopath too," he explained. He knew that she would be upset with him for not telling her sooner about his brush with death. "It took me a while to put the pieces together and get beyond the denial. You know, *see the forest for the trees*."

Joan decided to make light of the situation. Hanging her head in mock resignation, she put down the file and got in Yanni's face. "Remember me, Joan, college buddy and grad school chum. I deal with life and death almost everyday. Of course, I would have killed you for taking such risks, but I love you ol' buddy of mine." Then she planted a big smooch on Yanni's forehead.

Yanni looked up. He grinned and cocked his head from side to side as he reflected briefly on her lecture. Having successfully made her point,

Joan got out of Yanni's space. She went back to the nearby table to browse through the file of photos. A shiver went down her spine.

"Do you think that there may be a connection with Nicholas's desire to resurrect a dead relationship?" she asked Yanni.

"Yes," he answered. He put down his work resolutely and announced, "Let's go to dinner. I know a place where we can talk privately over a glass of wine and a solid meal."

"I'm game," Joan told him before grabbing a coat.

They took Yanni's car and stopped at a small cafe along the highway. Automatically, they slid into gender role-playing where they modeled a couple, rather than a straight woman and gay man. This kept their interactions away from prying eyes in public. Years ago, in college, they had learned when it was a time to rebel and a time to blend in. Under the present political climate, they found themselves preferring to mesh with present social conventions more frequently.

Yanni pressed the waitress for a secluded table by the window and they sat down. Immediately they ordered some wine and a vegetarian appetizer. He began his story, "I wasn't sure what I had until I developed the pictures much later. Then I analyzed them according to different dimensions. The merpeople validated my findings and led me to my conclusions. The bomb I found validated my suspicions, but I wasn't going to casually ask around for more information. Nicholas surfaced a month after my return to the states. I think he remembered that we hung together in college."

Joan placed her left hand on her head and looked down at her glass of Merlot. After rubbing her head briefly with graceful fingers, she glanced at Yanni.

"So it is only a matter of time before Nicholas surfaces again."

"Probably," Yanni speculated.

"Why couldn't you have just taken photos of drug-running aboard oil derricks in the Gulf?" Joan asked rhetorically. "You might be in less danger now."

"Because that is boring. Everyone who has a college degree from an ivy-league school knows that," Yanni asserted. "There's a bigger mystery here."

"Like what?" Joan questioned. Then she looked in Yanni's blue eyes and found her answer. It was the lure of the hunt that shone. Understanding that it was a hazard of his profession as a researcher, Joan conceded defeat, "Never mind. Now what?"

"Run like heck," he told her.

"How?" she asked politely.

"In so many ways," he answered.

"Got it," Joan said as she leaned back in her chair and eyed Yanni. She realized what a brilliant idea it had been to take up meditation and martial arts, much less, romance the instructor.

They finished their dinner and quickly paid. Joan placed her arm around Yanni's waist after they rose to leave. "I'll have to introduce you to my class. I think it best that I let Larry know about these connections. He may have some ideas. I'm gong to the cape next week."

"Send him my love, literally," Yanni requested with a light peck on Joan's cheek.

The next weekend, Joan told Larry about the conversation with Yanni. He thoughtfully nodded and added more information from his recent experiences.

"Donna, the graduate who accepted the lab position, seems to be on the run from a right-wing religious cult. Do you think her situation is related to all this?" Larry questioned while he and Joan walked on the wintery beach. A strong, cold wind compelled them to simultaneously turn around.

"It's too cold to be out," Joan observed. "Let's think about it over a cup of hot chocolate by a fire."

Briskly walking back to the bungalow, they made a light meal with hot chocolate. Then they took their refreshments to the living area and curled in each other's arms by the gas fire.

"Come to class tomorrow. I want you to meet Donna. See what you think," Larry proposed.

"I'd rather communicate with merpeople in another dimension," laughed Joan. "Sounds like Donna is very tough."

"Breeze in. Breeze out. Then check in with the merpeople, afterwards," Larry suggested.

"OK." Joan sighed, shrugging her shoulders at the distant horizon. "I'll give it all a whirl. I'd better go to bed early to rest up for tomorrow," she decided, seductively massaging his thigh.

Then she rose, stretched with a yawn, and left the room. Larry followed her into the bedroom. By the same time next evening, Joan sought the comfort of Larry's arms, reclining on the sofa with him.

"So what do you think?" he asked stroking her hair. "Somebody is looking out for her. The brochure that I gave her triggered a lot. You picked up on the symbology right away."

"She's connected to the Nicholas--earth spirit phenomenon. The man who gave you the brochure had a black dog with him. I don't know how it all fits together. As Yanni said, *it's a mystery.*"

"Any enlightened news from our friends in the other dimension?" Larry inquired.

"They confirmed that there is a connection. Same people running the three-ring circus," Joan quietly said.

"What's the game plan?" Larry asked her.

"Find out as much as we can to save ourselves and the planet," Joan advised. "Put our heads together with your lawyer friend, Eli, and Yanni."

"Being a geophysicist, I suggest we start with the story in the rock. What do you think is the significance of Nicholas' canary diamond?"

"I think that it is something like an identification badge. He only wanted it back after he knew I didn't want to run with his crowd. It comes from his mother's side of the family. So it must pertain to her connections. Aren't most underworld relationships passed down through the mother's side?"

"I suppose. Though I don't have personal experience with it. I'm just a vet from Viet Nam. If I had those connections, I never would have gone. I'd be careful about where you wear that stone in public. It might open doors that you don't want opened. Then we'd have to send your classmates out for you." Larry added with a grin.

"Maybe I could just meditate my way out." Joan chuckled.

"Certainly would be worth a try," her instructor recommended. "If they see you levitating they might run off."

"A friend in college said the stone had been used in astral projection," Joan continued in a concerned voice.

"Don't know if I'd want to get on that airship," Larry confessed.

"Maybe if I clean it, things might turn out differently. Transform the energy or something," Joan wistfully imagined out loud. "It is only a fancy rock."

"Sounds like more research."

"I have a few people in Maine that I can ask. People there are very spiritual, you know," Joan quipped. "Let's get to bed. This time I really am tired."

Larry rose from the couch and lifted her in his strong arms. He carried Joan to the bedroom and lightly placed her on the bed. Arousing her with soft kisses, he gently removed her clothes and lightly massaged her body. Tears rolled from her eyes as he warmed her. Kissing them away, he cradled her in his arms. She ran her fingers over his body and felt every muscle fiber and sinew in a loving caress. He took of his clothes and drew her next to him. He took her many places across the starry galaxy where she traveled until she fell to earth in a soft warmth unlike any she had ever experienced.

The next day he drove her to the Boston airport while they discussed Eli's investigation. They were puzzled by the threats over Donna's and Eli's life. Eli had been investigating a company for illegal hazardous waste.

"I have to let you go now," she told Larry before she departed. She gave him a short kiss at the gate.

"Not really," he replied, returning her affectionate peck on the cheek. "We will just pick up where we left off, except in this lifetime nothing will tear us apart."

Chapter Seven

The catastrophic loss of the feminine
In nature during the 1970's
Created a split in the tree of humanity

Tune Reference: *After The Gold Rush*

----Neil Young

WHEN JOAN TOLD Yanni about the interaction with Donna, he appeared perplexed. Something about the manufacturing company triggered his memory and his face paled Turning away from Joan, he shook his head.

"We are all vulnerable. Do you think the old holy roman empire is involved? It's connected to the Nicholas case as well as his ancestors," he told her as he finished chopping some vegetable he planned to stir fry for their dinner. Joan was staying the night at his apartment so they would have plenty of time to catch up without fear of eavesdroppers.

"Do you remember the time during the 1977 graduation when one hundred fifty seniors turned their backs on the Secretary of Defense?" Yanni questioned Joan. "They wanted to give him an honorary degree."

"Like the time when two-thirds of the Class of 1969 turned their backs on Henry Kissinger for the Viet Nam war," Joan recalled.

"Well, Nicholas never turned around. He applauded President Carter's Secretary of Defense," Yanni remembered.

"What does this have to do with the manufacturing company that tried to kill Donna in the field?"

"It is mind-control and the military-industrial complex," Yanni replied. "The President of Brown during World War II was also President of the Council of Foreign Relations or CFR during the Kennedy administration. I had to do research on this for a class of mine and found that JFK's press secretary wrote a letter in 1962, before the assassination, stating that Kennedy was not a member of the CFR. Even Schlesinger made a point to say that JFK had not been part of what he termed as the New York Establishment, which is a front for the military-industrial complex. It is a tax-write off, because it is a nonprofit."

Yanni heated some oil in a pan until it sizzled. He threw in the vegetables and quickly stir-fried them. Joan tended to the rice-cooker, which had almost completely steamed the brown rice.

"So what is the significance?" Joan asked.

"The next President of Brown University worked for the CIA during the Kennedy administration," Yanni added as he turned down the heat. He placed the stir fry in a bowl and placed it on the dining table.

Joan brought a bowl of rice to the table and poured cups of oolong tea for the two of them. Then they sat down to a candle light dinner as Yanni continued.

"After the Church Committee sent out their report around 1976, the President of Brown admitted by 1978 to having helped fund covert operations. Those covert operations involved mind control programs using drugs and torture. LBJ appointed him director of the National Endowment and Council on Humanities."

"I see," Joan said as she served herself and began savoring the stir fry. "This links Nicholas's drug-induced stalking to Donna's mentally-induced assailants. Eli said that the entire manufacturing company seemed to be off its rocker as if they were under hypnosis."

"The plot thickens," Yanni commented. "The Manurchian Candidate, himself, attended Brown during World War II along with some other members of the dirty dozen. He handled Oswald's handler. Oswald's handler had dated Jackie's mother during World War II. Jackie's mother later married a man who served in Naval Intelligence during WWII. Jackie, also, married a man who had been in Naval Intelligence during World War II. One of the Watergate burglars, E. Howard Hunt also attended Brown in the 1940's along with the head of the American Nazi Party. E. Howard Hunt ran the investigation into the Chappaquiddick incident. One of the reporters, who exposed the connection between Nixon and Watergate, had worked for Naval Intelligence as well. Now JFK, Jr attends Brown."

"That's like being in the hot seat," Joan observed.

"We got through it," Yanni insisted.

"I know." Then shaking her head, she remarked, "Except I am still being stalked by Nicholas and you were almost killed over finding an underwater world."

"You have a point," he acquiesced. "This labyrinth of our lives reminds me of the underwater creature in Casolaro's *Octopus*."

"I've read it," Joan answered. "So what?"

"Casolaro was investigating the satanic ritual abuse on the Cabazon Indian Reservation," Yanni pointed out. "He died under mysterious circumstances while investigating the many appendages of the *Octopus*. His research linked the abuse with things such as casinos, Roman empires, arms deals, drug deals, banking scams, backdoor spyware, biological and chemical warfare, and electromagnetic pulse generators."

"What else is new?" Then she thought for a moment before mentioning, "The electromagnetic pulse generators sound interesting. Let me guess, these generators do things like change the weather, knock out electronic technologies, alter brain waves, affect heart rhythms, and distort land masses."

"Some call it HARRP. The supporters claim that it is only a device for predicting the weather, but they are the only ones who believe that. HARRP is an acronym for High Frequency Active Auroral Research Program."

"If satanic cults are used to hide it, then it is no instrument of the celestials."

Yanni smiled playfully at Joan and placed some chopped yellow peppers between her lips. "Keep going!"

Joan quickly crunched the pepper in her mouth and remarked, "OK, so I can see the tentacles around me now. The herbalist was right-on with her perception. Now what about your island discovery? Where does that all come in?"

"I think it is being operated by the same dogs-of-war that are tracking Donna," Yanni speculated.

"The dogs of war are owned by the military-industrial complex. The military-industrial complex is owned by the financial backers for the Christian monarchy," Joan rambled.

"It is not a system of checks and balances. It is a dog-eat-dog world or a snake pit."

"At this point in history, the relationships are not balanced and are all codependent," Joan muttered. "This points to Nicholas."

Silence ensured as Yanni and Joan paused to reflect on their conversation while they finished eating.

"Let's go check on the merpeople," Yanni decided. "Maybe they have some insights into the dynamics of these relationships."

They took Yanni's car and drove to the closest beach. It was still early in the wintery evening and darkness hung over the ocean. Only the moon offered illumination over the black waters. Joan and Yanni got out of the car and peered into the distance. There in the silver hue of the moon's reflection swam several familiar figures.

"There they are," Joan whispered in an excited voice. She lightly tugged on Yanni's arm. Yanni smiled when he found them hovering at the water's surface.

"They can sense what we were discussing over dinner. They say that we are on the right track and that the world is in grave danger. We are to protect Eli and Donna as they notify the French Embassy about the use of nuclear plastics in world terrorism. The merpeople say that Donna's friend, Carrie, is a pivotal player in this world game. They are calling her a Queen, except this Queen knows how to walk off the chessboard in this latest Armageddon. Carrie knows how to change things to reset the balance of power. They say she is changing the balance of power even as we speak. The merpeople can sense this."

Chapter Eight

If you can't create a fantasy
You'll never find a reality

Tune Reference: *Perfect Lover*

----Kansas

"I THINK DONNA mentioned that Carrie majored in physics," Joan commented. "She's in the hospital now. Apparently the military-industrial-banking-christian-monarchy-holy roman empire complex threw a net over her. She has been caught, but Donna feels that Carrie will wiggle out of it somehow. If she can do this, then she is our woman."

"Maybe Carrie is more like Brier Rabbit in the briar patch." Yanni shook his head with a light chuckle. "Sometimes the small and defenseless have an easier time with thorny issues and turn them around for their own advantage."

"You may have a point there. Time will tell." Joan placed her hands on her hips and turned away from Yanni.

"They want us to pursue the history of the canary diamond on a deeper level," Yanni added, changing the subject.

"How?" Joan asked, refusing to look at Yanni in the eye.

"They indicate that the information will come to us," Yanni observed as he faced Joan and nodded towards the car.

"OK, let's go," she agreed, waving off the merpeople.

Once inside the vehicle, Yanni explained, "They don't want us hanging around the beach too long. Nicholas is still on the prowl."

"Why hasn't he figured out where you live?" Joan questioned as Yanni backed the car out of the parking lot. He headed for the main road back home.

"For one, it is secluded and has a security guard. Two, it is listed under my father's name, which is similar to my formal American name. It originally belonged to both of my parents and served as a haven for my Mother when she visited from Greece. I assumed ownership after college, but never bothered to change the listing. After finding the bomb on the plane, I decided to keep the listing as it is."

"What is your formal American name."

"James West, Jr.. You can see why I kept Yanni Stamas. It opens more doors in Greece."

They allowed the conversation to ebb like a dying fire and parted ways quietly. The next weekend, Joan traveled to the cape where Larry met and drove her to his beach bungalow. She unpacked her things and joined Larry in the living area. He carried in a tray with a pot of green tea and some finger foods.

"Eli is smitten with Donna," he announced setting the tray down on a dining table. The view from the dining table offered sweeping views of the cape. "He is taking her to the French Embassy with him. He's making his move while everybody believes he is dead."

Joan shook her head in disbelief at how fast events had progressed. "I saw the newspaper headlines on the way to work. They found his car in the cape."

"The body belongs to the man who stole his Carmen Ghia off the ferry dock," Larry explained.

"There's karmic justice for you," Joan observed, hiding an escaped tear from Larry. She turned away from him and stared out the window. "The merpeople communicated that we would need to help protect Eli and Donna during their visit to Washington D.C.."

"They seemed meant for each other," Larry commented as he handed Joan a cup of green tea.

"I agree," Joan said thoughtfully, accepting his offer as she faced him She carefully sipped the warm tea and reflected on the recent pace of events. "Where are all these quickening currents leading?"

"I don't know. I think that we will know more after Eli visits Washington D. C. with Donna," Larry speculated. "They are leading to a confrontation with the military-industrial-banking-christian-monarchy-holy roman empire complex."

"That's a mouthful. I'll do what I can to shift the balance with the homeopathics. I think I can come up with one for Donna when she is ready," Joan proposed.

"I'll make sure Donna's classmates sharpen their ninja skills," Larry decided with a hint of chagrin. "They are getting a workout relaying messages between myself, Eli, and Donna while remaining invisible to the rest of the world. They will be on standby for the trip to Washington D.C.."

"What's Donna's connection to the Black Dog group?"

"I'm not sure. I think it may have something to do with her friend Carrie, the one who seems to have a pivotal role."

"Whatever *that* is!" Joan exclaimed as she waved her hand across her face as if to brush all the recent events away. She reached for a kalamata olive for her pita bread and hummus.

Larry chuckled at her words. Then he shuddered and tried to shake off the fear that surfaced through his thoughts. Joan watched him and tried to imagine what had caused a shiver in Larry. She shook her head and munched on another slice of the pita bread. Lifting her eyes to study the ceiling, she sensed that her frame of reference differed from Larry's. Focused on moving forward, she determined to avoid emoting.

Larry received a frantic call from Eli to have someone meet Donna at the Boston airport. She had been pursued in Washington D.C. and had fled from the National Mall after a tip-off involving a black dog. They separated and a taxi took Donna directly to the airport. Several of Donna's classmates picked her up at the Boston airport and whisked her away from several men who seemed to be waiting for her arrival. They got her safely back to her studio apartment without being detected.

Larry called Joan to tell her about the trip to Washington D.C.. "Eli asked Donna to marry him afterwards," he told her.

"Good for them. They had a trial by fire!"

"The wedding is set for the Fall. Eli wants to have it in Maine by his favorite waterfall. I hiked there last summer. Save the date for October 23rd. It is a bright spot in all this intrigue," Larry added.

"Great!" Joan heartily agreed. "I know that area. It's near the ocean and the views are spectacular. I'll see you next weekend and we can make more specific plans."

She hung up the phone after telling Larry, "I love you." She declined to tie the knot with anyone right now. Their lives remained in a tremendous state of flux. The summer continued uneventfully. Nobody saw Nicholas again, though a prevailing sense of eeriness told them that they were energetically being tracked somehow.

By October, Carrie had wiggled her way out of the hospital predicament and came to Woodsport to attend Donna's wedding. Exactly how she managed to escape eluded Joan and Donna remained silent on the details. Sensing that the topic was still to painful for Donna to discuss, Joan gave her time and didn't press for details. Instead, Joan continued to watch and wait like a ship's captain scanning the horizon for sailing portents. She felt that it was important to keep flowing with life events rather than get bogged down. People could resume picking up the pieces of their lives later. For the moment, they kept moving forward. Joan observed that Donna never moved back to her family's cottage and remained in the studio apartment near her friends and protective classmates. While Carrie escaped, her past, Donna ran from it, and Joan continued to hold steady as if she was holding a protective space for the three of them. Joan seized the opportunity to pick up Carrie at the airport. She hoped to learn more about this mysterious friend of Donna's, who the merpeople highly recommended. The trip with both Carrie and Donna might elucidate the reason that their lives so rapidly converged. After meeting Carrie at the airport, Donna and Joan drove to Maine for the wedding.

"I'm so happy to finally get a chance to meet you," Joan told Carrie as she drove along the highway in the privacy of her vehicle. They had kept introductions brief at the Boston airport to avoid being noticed.

"I wouldn't miss Donna's wedding for the world," Carrie replied with a light grin. "Donna has told me what a great help you have been in the whole process."

"Carrie's going back to school this upcoming term to complete her physics degree," Donna announced as she lightly changed the subject.

"A physics major, huh!" Joan nodded at Donna, who sat beside her in the passenger seat. Donna evaded her glance and stared out the window. She ended their small talk with silence.

"Yes, a physics major," Carrie answered quietly as she curiously watched the interaction between the two women in the front seat.

"I have a canary diamond that I'd like to have you check out. I want your opinion as a physicist," Joan mentioned. She glanced in her rear-view mirror to note Carrie's glib reaction.

Donna shrugged. With a toss of her head, she indicated her disinterest and lack of commitment to Joan's pursuit. Joan and Larry had already shown her the stone when the truth of their love affair came out. The rest of the class remained in the dark about the relationship, which probably would remain undetected until they received a wedding invitation from the covert couple. As for the canary diamond, Donna could tell that it had been infused with a particular frequency, but she could not focus on the origin. The significance of the stone eluded them. Joan would need to continue to work on transmuting the energy associated with the canary diamond with help from her homeopath and herbalist.

When they reached the site of the waterfall, Joan dropped Donna and Carrie off at a nearby hotel and left to meet Yanni at his research laboratory thirty miles south.

"How was the drive to Maine?" he asked as Joan greeted him with a light kiss on the cheek and hug.

"Too quiet," she told him.

Yanni laughed softly. "That's what happens when you travel with people who have been on the run."

Joan smiled. "I suppose. Carrie is watching everything. She is very bright and doesn't miss a beat. She seems to be tracking something energetically from the depths of her soul. It's as if she already senses her place in all of this. Now I can understand now how the merpeople are able to track her. She is so intact."

"Can't wait to meet her," Yanni said as he continued working with his photos and laboratory analysis. "This wedding is bringing us all together in a very interesting and synchronistic way."

"Yes, I know. There seems to be more at play here. Meet you at the apartment later this afternoon. I'll make dinner tonight. I'm on call for the hospital for the next twenty-four hours, so I need to get some rest."

The next evening, Joan and Yanni met Larry moments before the wedding at the top of the waterfall. He stood surrounded by Ei's colleagues from Washington D. C., MIT, and the EPA. Larry had spent the previous day entertaining Eli's closest friends who kept his secret. Even Eli's relatives thought he was dead. Likewise, nobody showed from his former law firm in Boston.

"This is just like a scene from a Carlos Castenada book," Larry whispered as he observed the waterfall while the couple exchanged vows. "Rivers represent consciousness."

"I think that is also a Jungian concept," Joan replied in a hushed voice. "Eli has had a shaman's death. He died in one world and has transcended in the next life."

Larry smiled with a nod. Joan moved closer to whisper in his ear, "Most couples honeymoon by some source of water. I call it the Niagara Falls archetype."

With those words, Larry raised his head with a silent chuckle and put his arm around Joan, who quietly resumed watching the wedding ceremony. Nobody noticed the group of men standing around one swarthy man who had his binoculars focused on the wedding party. They stood behind a grove of trees on a nearby cliff. Suddenly Joan raised her head from Larry's shoulder with a light wince. She looked around the terrain, but Nicholas had already stepped back into the cliff's shadows.

"What's wrong?" Larry asked quietly. Joan's face had turned pale for brief moment.

"I just had a horrible feeling that Nicholas showed up," she answered as she slipped away from the group for the closest building where the reception would be held minutes later. "I am getting chilled."

Larry followed her to the ballroom. Together they sat down at one of the tables and assessed the environment. Everything seemed to be in order. Soon the rest of the wedding party joined them. They danced and celebrated throughout the evening without any more signs of Nicholas. After the reception, the newly married couple left for their cottage below the waterfall. Carrie and Joan chatted with Larry and two colleagues from a renowned technical institute.

"It is great to see Eli so happy," Dan, the biologist with Eli's investigation, remarked to the others. He had been on vacation in Maine ever since the lead scientist of their group had been suicided, an occurrence that had happened after a meeting with a journalist from a popular magazine. Although the medical examiner ruled the death a suicide, those involved with

Eli's investigation were convinced that the scientist had been murdered. Like the newly-married couple, a significant number of those in the wedding party also maintained a low public profile.

"Did you bring the canary diamond?" Carrie asked Joan. She quickly changed the subject before the conversation became too serious for a wedding party. Carrie could sense a different vibrational quality around Joan's body and had wondered why.

"How did you know?" Joan answered her with a question.

"Something about you seems different from when I met you at the airport," Carrie informed her.

Joan shuddered, recalling her thoughts about Nicholas during the ceremony. Without a word, she quickly produced the canary diamond from her purse and placed it on the table in front of her. Larry grinned and nodded his approval. Carrie could hold her own with Joan.

"It's a tracking device," Carrie observed without touching the canary diamond.

Joan's face turned pale. Larry noticed and put his arm around her, pulling her towards him. She rubbed her left hand over her head as if trying to erase any memory of Nicholas.

Observing Joan's immediate reaction to her words, Carrie said in a soft voice as she held the object in her right hand, "But look, the stone is also an illumination tool."

Joan's hand fell softly from her forehead as she watched the canary diamond glow in Carrie's palms. "How did you do that?"

The rest of the scientists at the table watched the stone light up in Carrie's hand like magic.

"Physics," Carrie replied. Then she noticed the quizzical expression on Joan's face and explained. "It is an object that responds to frequencies in other dimensions. It has been programmed."

"Is it safe?" Joan asked.

"I don't know. I never considered the question until now. I never learned to ask those kinds of questions in my physics classes. Instead we just study the phenomenon and figure out the danger part later." Stunned by the gravity of the situation, she returned the stone to Joan, "Here, you hold it."

The canary diamond glowed in Joan's palms. She passed the stone around the group and every scientist was able to make the stone glow. Everyone felt awed by the experience. After a moment's reflection, they looked at Carrie for further explanation.

"Let's take the canary diamond on a hike tomorrow morning and see if we can find the portal that is connecting us to these other dimensions," Carrie suggested. "There must be several in this area."

"Oh, you mean like an alternative reality?" Kevin asked. He worked as a mathematician on Eli's investigation.

"I don't know how alternative it is yet, though it does seem to be a reality," Carrie quipped.

The group left the reception room and walked back to their hotel rooms a few hundred yards across the highway. The scientists dropped Carrie off at her door and wished her good night. Joan and Larry entered another room down the hall.

They met at the top of the waterfall the next morning. Yanni arrived first and greeted the others.

"Joan called me last night and told me to show up." He laughed when Carrie offered him a puzzled glance. He had left the reception early and missed the discussion about the glowing canary diamond. "She said to be ready for a hike."

Joan and Larry were the last ones to join the group collecting near the waterfall.

"Let's see if you pass the rock test," Joan said as she placed the canary diamond inside Yanni's palm.

"You know, this is beginning to resemble a geology field trip," remarked Larry with a lighthearted grin.

"Hey look, he passes," Joan announced.

Everyone crowded around Yanni to see the glowing stone inside his hand. Yanni remained speechless as he gazed at the phenomenon. Then he looked seriously at Carrie as he handed the stone to her with a light jest. "Here, you are the Magician-Queen. Take us to the other dimension."

With a shrug, Carrie glanced at Joan instead. Joan eagerly nodded and encouraged her to take the lead. Everyone else in the group smiled at her and adjusted the loading straps on their backpacks.

Carrie gazed at the Atlantic Ocean in the distance behind the group as she turned her back to the waterfall.

"OK, we are in the presence of three different portals leading to various dimensions. One is on the other side of the waterfall near that cliff over there. I saw some men with binoculars standing there yesterday during the wedding."

Joan gasped with the realization that she had most likely been stalked again by Nicholas.

"Let's skip that one for now," Larry insisted as Joan collected her wits.

"OK. The other two seem to be where the water from the falls meets the Atlantic."

"I know that trail," Yanni piped. "There are a couple of caves at the base of the cliff. They can only be reached at low tide.

Without any more hesitation, Yanni turned and started walking towards the trail that lead to the base of the cliff. Carrie continued to hold the stone in her palm and followed Yanni. The rest of the group walked behind them. An hour later, they had found the caves at the end of the trail. Carrie held the glowing stone in the direction of each cave. A blue light emerged out of the cave to her right.

"There's our portal. I wouldn't trust the other ones," she observed.

"The merpeople are waving us on," Yanni commented as he stared at the Atlantic's horizon.

Half of the six-member hiking group were staring out at the sea. Carrie glanced at the scientists. They merely shrugged when Larry and Joan agreed with Yanni.

"People in these parts are pretty spiritual," Kevin commented.

With a hint of reluctance, Carrie walked inside the cave with the blue light.

"I don't think we'll be needing any flashlights, especially since I didn't bring one," Carrie observed with chagrin. Her focus remained on the energetics of the lighted cave, which resonated with the glow of the canary diamond.

The rest followed Carrie. Two hundred yards inside the cave, the blue light increased in intensity, almost seeming to arise from the rock walls of the cave. The group remained content with their own thoughts until Joan broke the silence.

"It's beautiful!" Joan exclaimed as her hands ran over the glowing walls.

"It's selenite," Larry observed.

One mile inside the cave, they arrived at a subterranean world. Carrie sat down on one of the selenite boulders and gazed at the environment. Trees and bushes glowed a multitude of colors. Fairies soared in the air over the flowers. Dazzling sprays of light dripped off their wet wings and graced the plants below them. Elegant furry-winged dragons soared in the distant skies over a giant metropolis.

"The portal leads to the MidEarth," Larry observed as he studied the scene around him.

"And the fallen city of Atlantis," Yanni added.

"As well as a collection of biological species that have been mythologized," Dan rejoined.

"My vote is for the alternative reality," Kevin told Carrie with a grin.

This time Kevin assumed leadership for the hike and made his way to the fallen city of Atlantis. Carrie rose from the selenite boulder and quietly followed behind the group. Something about their present experience resonated in their souls, juxtaposing against the flat dimensional world where they had been pursued. Their lives had suddenly found a depth and meaning that they had never known before. Yet, in the recesses of an ancient memory, they understood that hey were only revisiting a world of essences they had known before.

At the entrance to the metropolis stood a circular Mayan calendar surrounding by an array of giant crystals.

"And here is the time machine to go with my alternative reality," Kevin remarked as he surveyed the arrangement. "I vote that we don't activate it."

"You must have read my thoughts," Yanni agreed. He stood next to Kevin and studied the arrangement.

"I'm ready to head back," Carrie ventured in a low voice. The canary diamond had begun to buzz in her palms. Feeling slightly dizzy by the effect, she noted the beginnings of information-overload surfacing in her conscious state. "I can come back later and bring a bigger lunch."

"Me too," Joan acknowledged, smiling at Carrie's dry sense of humor. Nobody had packed a lunch. Everyone munched on energy bars, nuts, and fruit.

"The canary diamond is buzzing. Those men around the portal on the cliff may be near," Carrie warned.

"OK, I'm coming," Larry said, after watching Joan shiver at the thought of meeting Nicholas again.

"I'm going," Dan rejoined, recalling his reason for hiding in Maine.

"Me too," Kevin added. "We've come this far. Let's not blow it by overdoing it."

The group headed for the cave leading back to the beach. Joan gave one last glance at the furry dragons soaring in the sky.

"You know, they really do breathe fire," she observed, wondering about the physiology required to support such a biological adaptation.

"That is what happens when you drink from those subterranean rivers of lava," Dan said. The group turned and noticed the red streams of molten lava climbing the far walls of the terrain. The furry dragons were hovering over the region like bees around a flower.

"It's the true meaning of fire water," Yanni commented. Indigenous cultures used the term fire water for alcohol.

"Supposedly dragons were around during some of the most volcanic periods of the Earth's history. Maybe that is all there was to drink, lava," Dan reasoned. "Who knows?"

"The local herbalist tells a story about a Hawaiian flower essence company that lost a cofounder to Pele. Pele is the Hawaiian goddess of the volcano. Apparently this cofounder was not respectful in the way he made the essences and Pele drove him to commit suicide."

"Do you think Pele is here?" Yanni asked.

"In one way or the other, Pele guards the spirit of the earth," Joan explained. "I think that we just found the spirit of the earth and must continue to harmonize with it."

"What do you think that means?" Larry questioned.

"I don't know," Joan admitted. "But, I suspect that we will find out in a few years."

The group made it safely out of the portal before dusk. They walked back to the hotel and decided to bring Eli and Donna on tomorrow's morning excursion.

"Let's talk about it over dinner," Joan proposed before they went back to their rooms to relax and freshen up.

A few hours later, they drove to a nearby restaurant with vegetarian fare and discussed their experiences.

"Eli and Donna are a go. They are very excited about the discovery," Larry announced once everyone had gathered at the table. "They sorta expected that their honeymoon might get cut short for some reason or another. At least this a positive change."

Carrie handed the stone back to Joan. "I don't know how much time we have before Nicholas and his associates track our findings. I want you to learn how to read the stone so that you can detect Nicholas' presence more objectively. Also, you may need it to find other portals and avoid negative ones."

"You are right," Joan told her. "For all we know, tomorrow may be our last time in the cave, so we should make the most out of it."

"Let's see what we can learn. Some of the brightest minds in the world are at this table tonight. Put them to work," Larry proposed.

Kevin and Dan grinned.

"We survived this far," Dan repeated.

"One big question remains," Yanni began, changing the conversation to employ the intellectual talent at the table. "How much does Nicholas's relations know about these portals?"

"The canary diamond is apparently a family heirloom," Joan surmised.

"Maybe that is why they wanted you in the family," Carrie guessed. "Maybe their use of it was limited. Maybe they only know about the negative portals rather than the MidEarth one. Only someone with an internal light source would be able to create a light strong enough to resonate with the earth's spirit. It takes more than just illumination. You've got to have an independent light source."

"You know, I think Carrie is right, even though I don't understand everything she just said," Larry commented.

"I think Nicholas's relations can detect the MidEarth, which is probably why his family began drilling in this area. Those oil rigs off the coast belong to his relatives," Joan interjected.

"The rock layers to the MidEarth must be thinner in this region than most others on the planet," Larry commented.

Kevin interrupted them, "The other big question is what does all this have to do with Eli's investigation of the company making nuclear plastics?"

"I suspect it is the same group behind both. They want to ultimately control world resources and will even resort to nuclear blackmail to accomplish this objective," Dan said, fighting off a nervous twitch in his left eye.

Those sitting around the table realized the gravity of Dan's words and reflected silently for a moment. After some lighter conversation, the group drove back to the hotel and retired early for the night. They met Donna and Eli at the trailhead the next day. The couple seemed lighter, brighter, and ready to get down to business. They followed directly behind Larry, who led the hiking party to the caves on the beach. Swiftly, they made their way past the selenite crystals and to the subterranean world. Donna began immediately deciphering the history of the place as she toured the vacant metropolis and studied the rock layers.

"I am getting that three distinct groups that came together before Atlantis fell. One group called the Serpentines possessed a reptilian appearance which they cleverly masked to fool the others. Another group consisted of Lemurians from the planet Mu. The third group pertained to the other intergalactic refugees as well as the earth and water spirits."

They followed Donna around the metropolis as she investigated the terrain. Joan examined a blackened stone room, which appeared charred from a fire.

"This room once housed an enormous crystal, which was destroyed to protect the planet from mind control," Joan observed, running her hands over the rocks. "You can see the fragments in the center."

Then she gazed over the roofless metropolis at the far end of the walls of the cavern. "The fragments in that wall appear to those of a meteorite, probably from the one that sunk Atlantis after the protective crystal grids were destroyed."

"Great history lesson," Dan said as he pointed a gun at Joan and ordered everyone to line up on the nearby wall.

The rest of the group complied. Then he said to Joan, "Hand over the canary diamond."

She tossed the canary diamond at his feet. Dan picked up the diamond and put it into a cloth bag along with a fairy that he had snagged earlier. Suddenly a loud rumble echoed across the top of the cavern as rocks fell from the ceiling.

Carrie began to feel lightheaded and weak as she realized that the noise came from the drilling on the oil rigs. Tapping into the earth's spirit seemed to affect her as well. She slumped to the ground as her legs gave out underneath her. Dan seemed not to notice her reaction to the drilling, while he focused on containing the frantic fairy inside the cloth bag. Joan remained quiet. She watched Carrie completely pass out on the stone floor. She sensed that Dan intended to kill them before he left so that no one else would know about the portal.

A furry dragon appeared overhead and landed between Carrie's body and Dan. "Let go of the fairy," the furry dragon communicated in a silent voice.

"How did you know about the fairy?" Dan asked out loud.

"The woman dying on the ground told me," the furry dragon, answered, breathing fire at Dan's feet. He dropped the cloth bag as he screamed in pain. The fairy escaped and flew away.

"When did Nicholas pay you off?" Joan sternly questioned him. The look of shock on her face had given away to anger.

"He met me in my hotel room after the wedding," Dan cried before the furry dragon torched him.

"Did he pay you to kill the lead scientist and make it look like a suicide?" Eli quizzed, seizing the moment to interrogate their failed attacker.

"Yes!" he uttered with a final menacing voice. His body disappeared behind the smoke and flames.

The rest of the furry dragons breathed fire at the metal drill rod that had penetrated the wall of the ceiling. The metal melted into the ceiling and the drilling ceased. The furry dragon left the group to join the others. Joan reached for Carrie and tried to revive her. They carried Carrie out of the metropolis and placed her by a shimmering stream near the edge of the colorful forest. The fairies encouraged Joan to moisten Carrie's lips and forehead with water from the stream. Carrie slowly opened her eyes as she regained her strength.

"That's quite a connection that you have with the earth spirit in the MidEarth," Donna told Carrie as she held her hand.

"I dreamed that I flew on the back of one of the furry dragons," she confessed.

"Must have the been the dragon that burned Dan and saved us," Joan observed.

"Let's get out of here before Nicholas and his international group traps us," Larry urged them.

Eli nodded and took Donna's other hand to help her rise. Kevin helped Carrie to her feet and assisted her until she regained the strength in her legs. Once outside of the cave, they hurried back to the hotel and checked out. Eli paid for Dan's hotel bill and left a fake forwarding address for Nicholas to pursue. The canary diamond remained in the MidEarth, where Nicholas would never be able to retrieve it.

Chapter Nine

Wouldn't it be great

If all the weapons

In the world

Turned into balloons

And became our dreams

Of freed loved ones?

Tune Reference: *Ninety-Nine Red Balloons*

----Nena

TIME PASSED QUICKLY as everyone went separate ways. Early in the summer of 1983, Joan received a letter from Carrie. Her husband, Brent, had accepted a research position with a university in Rhode Island, where he planned to pursue a Doctorate in Physics. They planned to move at the end of the summer after Carrie completed her BA in Physics and Brent finished his internship. Carrie planned to take a few months off before deciding between getting a job or going back to school. Joan expressed delight at the opportunity to see more of Carrie and her husband. Her old alma mater was close to the university. She often visited the area to take continuing education courses there.

After the experience with the MidEarth portal, the group had quietly dispersed and returned to their individual affairs across the nation. Carrie went back to Texas where she went to college and married the young man that she had been dating. Kevin eventually finished his sabbatical and resumed work with another research lab. Donna and Ei found a larger studio apartment on the cape where they continued to work on their projects. On weekends and holidays, the couple returned to the honeymoon cottage near the waterfall. Eli resumed his investigation while Donna continued to work as a consulting geophysicist at Woodsport. They kept close contact with all their friends from the wedding. Yanni maintained his low profile and continued his research at the Institute. Larry and Joan conducted their short distance relationship while researching their experiences with the portals and keeping up with their day jobs.

Later that Fall, Joan attended a conference at her alma mater. She drove straight to the campus and arranged to go with Carrie afterwards for dinner. The prospect of seeing a familiar face after a full day of class, helped Joan feel balanced and centered. She hoped to spend more time getting to know Carrie and her life partner. Unfortunately, Brent stayed at the research lab that evening and could not join them. Joan and Carrie agreed to meet at an art gallery on the Brown campus. They wished to avoid calling attention to their encounter while avoid waiting for each other in the cold and rain. The art gallery not only offered shelter from the elements but would make any wait even more enjoyable, in the event someone was detained. The women agreed to meet each other near the British sword collection, because it was the most striking exhibit and easiest to find.

"How was the seminar?" Carrie asked when Joan strolled by the exhibit.

"It is interesting," Joan responded with a slightly dazed look on her face from information overload. "Let's get something to eat. It has been a long day."

As the two women turned away from the sword collection, a man dressed as a 17th century French knight suddenly appeared from behind the glass displays.

"Can I answer any questions on the swords for you?" he asked Carrie and Joan.

Joan stopped abruptly and looked quizzically at the man in costume. He had a big white cross on his red tunic. Carrie focused on the swords in one of the cases and selected one for discussion.

"Tell us about this one." Carrie requested as she pointed to an ornate sword that seemed to match the man's costume. The sword had a similar cross on the hilt.

"Oh, that one belongs to me," he said. "I am French knight of the Order of Malta. I had to give it up after Napoleon came to Malta. Alas."

Joan chuckled. "So what brings you and your sword to Rhode Island?"

"I came to the Isle of Rhodes to search for my roots among the Templar knights," he graciously replied with a bow.

"This is Rhode Island," Carrie told him with a straight face.

The Knight shook and bowed his head again, "Oh, I am only off by a few hundred years backwards."

"That's OK," Joan interjected, before confronting the knight. "You are only looking in *A Distant Mirror*.

Carrie flashed Joan a puzzled look, recognizing the title from a book by Barbara Tuchman. She watched Joan carefully for further information.

"Yes, I see," the Knight responded as his head sunk lower and lower into his chest. Then he growled a threat to the women, "The Grays will return. That is all I can say."

He raised his forearm, which was covered in armor. Joan nudged Carrie quickly away from the knight before he struck them. They hurried down the hall and walked briskly past the guard at the exit. Twilight had settled on the campus and the women felt a shiver in the air.

"Let's get out of here before an army follows us," Joan urged. "I know a place down the road where we can get a bite to eat."

Carrie silently walked with Joan to the small cafe almost a half mile away. A waiter seated them at a small table in a quiet corner. They quickly ordered tea and an appetizer before politely waving the waiter off.

"That knight came unglued when you mentioned Barbara Tuchman's book," Carrie remarked as she looked Joan squarely in the eye.

"I know. I suspected that he might," Joan said, pulling away from Carrie's stare. "I caught him lying."

"Which lie did you catch?" Carrie asked with a perplexed look on her face.

"The one about his roots with the Templars. According to *A Distant Mirror*, the Templars were politically ravaged until there was nothing left. Not that I am totally a fan of the Templars," she added. "There were no true successors in this medieval dog fight for world domination regardless whether it was by military might or religious intolerance."

Satisfied with her explanation, Carrie relaxed a little in her chair when the waiter returned with herb tea and appetizers. She told him to return later for their order, then she resumed questioning Joan after he left. "You metaphorically placed a mirror in his face like you were unmasking a vampire."

"I know," Joan admitted with a shrug as she leaned across the table. She sensed that Carrie would not quit until she had found her answer.

Whatever that was, only Carrie would know. Joan continued, "My mother went to garden parties with Barbara Tuchman. I knew about her books before I went to the university."

"JFK referred to Tuchman as a National Treasure," Carrie commented. "He used *Guns of August* like it was the bible for the Cuban Missile Crisis. One of the themes that emerges from these two books is the existence of an elite group of warriors with nothing better to do but make war. The economic survival of this class in society depends on war. It is a polite way of mirroring the military industrial complex, except by October of 1962, the dogs of war had gone rabid."

"It is bigger than that," Joan quietly told her. "You heard the man: the Grays will return. The conflict is intergalactic."

Carrie waved her arms in the air with a mock sigh. "Don't get spacey on me."

Joan laughed at her play on words. Even though Carrie could be a firebrand, she possessed a dry sense of humor. Carrie dropped her comic gesticulations and smiled at Joan.

"Who are the Grays?" Carrie deadpanned.

"Fallen Light Beings associated with the rabid dogs of war," Joan replied. "Some hardcore Nazis contacted them through occultism."

"What makes you think that our Knight of Malta wasn't on cannabis?" Carrie questioned.

Joan sensed Carrie's concerned. After pausing to reflect for brief moment, she agreed, "Yes, I understand your point. During the Crusades, the elite warriors used hash to attain a level of consciousness where they could kill without thinking. The Knights of Malta controlled the spice routes so that their cultivated assassins would have plenty of mind-altering drugs. The word assassins comes from the word 'hash' and pertains to the Hashishan sect or Ismaili. Contemporaries like Francis of Assisi dropped out of the Crusades and sought spiritual enlightenment with the natural high of compassion, whereas others purposely promoted dissociation to commit ritual murder."

"This sect still exists today. In the Southwest, we call them the *nadas*. Some are convinced that they are the remnant dark agents in the *Lord of the Rings Trilogy*."

"In their dissociative states, these organizations seek communication with the Grays."

"OK, I can buy that. After WWII, the Grays infiltrated our national space programs as well as US politics. Who needs to vote with the Hashishans around!" Looking down at the cleared table, she changed the subject, "Let's order. I think I'll have a cup of clam chowder," Carrie said as she looked up at the waiter. He had just returned to take their requests. She switched to a less controversial topic for the moment and then resumed once he departed. Leaning over the table, Carrie questioned Joan further, "What do you mean by occultism and rabidity?"

"The Thule Society and then some. Larry and I have been doing our homework since the hike to MidEarth." Joan gazed into Carrie's blue eyes. "You do remember, don't you?"

"I'm trying to forget," she thoughtfully replied. No one had talked about their experiences in the portal. They had just picked up the pieces the best they could and went separate ways. Carrie leveled with Joan's gaze. "There is so much of my life that I have tried to forget that the portal experience got tossed-in with all the other painful memories."

"Maybe this one just needs to be reframed," Joan told her softly. "We survived with the memories of the fascinating MidEarth." Then she leaned back and began eating her vegetable stir fry. "And it proved very inspiring."

Carrie wiped away a small hot tear as Joan looked down at her plate. Joan pretended not to notice the tear. She could not imagine the depths of Carrie's thoughts and feelings.

Carrie smiled slightly. "I think you are right."

She sipped her tea and calmed herself. Joan remained quiet for a moment and waited for Carrie to begin eating. After a few spoonfuls of soup, Carrie added, "Donna has been investigating ley lines with her latest geophyical survey. She found an ancient communication network embedded in the rocks of different formations."

"Has she ever thought about using them to stabilize the planet?" Joan asked.

"Do you mean use the gridding pattern to deal with geopathic stress like earthquakes?" Carrie questioned her for clarification.

"Why not?"

"Hmm, the geophysics industry is mostly owned by the oil companies and religious societies," Carrie observed. "The oil companies own the alternative energy industry, especially the photovoltaic sector and fuel cells. They plan on drilling more extensively in the Gulf, which Donna suspects will unhinge the planet. Stability is worth a try."

"Sounds like they are trying to poison the planet," Joan remarked. "Larry and I learned that the Grays had been part of the intergalactic wars of ancient Egypt. There were some references to them in the books we found."

"Information overload," Carrie pleaded softly as she gazed at her bowl of chowder. "So the occults of the Holy Roman Empire run the energy and geophysics industry, while the Grays are behind the aeronautics."

"It is an another Armageddon waiting to happen."

They continued eating in silence and paid the waiter before walking to Joan's car parked on campus. The night sky remained clear and they could easily find the constellations of Orion and Cassiopeia. Twinkling brightly above the city lights, the stars soothed whatever terror remained in the women's consciousness.

"Brent will be home late tonight. He has night duty. They are collecting data from photometers on top of one of the tallest dorms," Carrie told her as she got in the car beside Joan. "We could go check up on him. He'll appreciate the leftover clam chowder."

Joan smiled. "Let's go."

They found their way across town to the University. Inside the computer lab, Brent huddled over a large workstation and typed intently.

"Working away?" Carrie asked as she warmly kissed him and handed him a doggie bag.

Brent smiled with a nod, before peering inside the doggie bag and happily smacking his lips. "Oh thank you so much," he said as he rose from his chair to retrieve a computer printout. "It will be my midnight snack. It's going to be awhile before I get home. They need this data by next week."

Carrie glanced at Joan and let her know that she was ready to go. "OK, don't work too hard. We're going back home. I'm tired and it has been a long day."

Then Joan and Carrie left the room and walked back to the car.

"He is a hard worker," Joan observed as she turned the key into the ignition.

Carrie sighed before she explained. "He's brilliant, though he hides from the world in his work."

They returned to the apartment and went straight to bed. Brent made it home after midnight and slept in the next day. After breakfast, he hurried back to the computer lab to finish his assignment.

"Come visit me in Maine," Joan told Brent before he left.

Brent grinned and waved her off. "Maybe during spring break."

Joan laughed lightly at his manner. He seemed to be floating on air.

Carrie waved good-bye and laughed too. After he left, Carrie turned towards Joan and said truthfully, "I just don't see him getting away soon. There is an even bigger project coming up. I tease him that the computer will eat his brain, but he ignores me."

"Well, keep in touch. I gotta go now myself," Joan announced as she hugged Carrie.

Carrie nodded and promised, "We'll talk more soon."

Chapter Ten

Signs of the end of the world

Echo in the silent dark streets

And the neon lights

That most people no longer hear

Because what is being said is only heard

By the lonely who look for other visions

Tune Reference: *The Sounds Of Silence*

----Paul Simon and Art Garfunkel

THE NEXT MONTH Carrie drove with Donna to visit Joan in Maine. Joan and Carrie had not talked since her trip to Rhode Island. For that matter, the group as a whole still had barely processed the experience with MidEarth. Life events kept them busy and their understanding of the event remained limited. Joan hoped that the get-together might provide the opportunity to collate the information at a deeper level. Both she and Larry sensed that they needed to achieve greater depth in their perception, but they could not get there. Yet, some sense of urgency pushed them forward as if their lives depended on it. This compulsion puzzled them and they groped for more ways to gain clarity.

The two women stayed with Joan at her cottage. On this wintery day, they took a short hike after arriving in the early afternoon. They found several inches of fresh snow on the path and the walk became strenuous.

When the snow began to fall heavily, their steps became even more difficult. They trudged on for another half mile and then turned around. By the time they returned to the cottage, they were thoroughly exhausted. After a shower and change of clothes, they prepared a light meal and huddled around the woodstove in Joan's living room. The combination of exercise, hydrotherapy, and nourishment broke down communication barriers. As a result the women began to reflect on their past experiences and brainstorm on the meaning of it all.

"I still wonder about those furry dragons that we found in the MidEarth," Donna said, breaking the silence.

Carrie reclined on the oval braid rug and gazed at the ceiling looking as if she was studying the stars in the sky. She said softly, "They were from another civilization."

Joan stared at the fire, and added in a half-daze, "You're right, Carrie."

Donna looked at one woman and then the next as if to quickly absorb their thoughts. Then she proposed another question, "OK, so what civilization and when?"

"The Dragon flyers," Carrie replied with a half smirk before she playfully threw a pillow at Donna.

Joan broke her gaze from the hearth and smiled in amusement as Donna caught the pillow and joined Carrie on the floor. Donna rested beside Carrie and looked at the ceiling as if wanting to see what Carrie was seeing. After a brief moment of reflection, Donna announced, "Got it."

Joan remained silent, continuing to watch the interplay between the two women with amusement. They were almost childlike in the way they played with ideas and related to each other without bias or ego.

"You were a Dragon flyer in your past life," Donna observed as she continued to eyeball the ceiling along with Carrie.

"So the furry dragons that we saw were survivors from that civilization. The furry dragon still connected to Carrie, although Carrie only flew the furry dragon in her dream. The furry dragon sensed your condition and perceived the drilling as a threat," Joan surmised, thinking out loud so that the others could add their own two bits. "Did you approach the furry dragon in your semiconscious state, Carrie?" "Or did the furry dragon just decide to come and save us?"

"I communicated our need to him in my dream," Carrie answered. "I didn't ask or command. We had another type of bond and I went to him for aid like it was automatic. Like I knew about his capabilities from somewhere before."

"The furry dragon responded immediately," Joan commented with a slight shudder at the thought of what would have occurred without the intervention. "It threw Dan off his rocker with the element of surprise. He confessed to everything."

"Nothing like a lawyer to elicit a confession from the doomed," Donna stated dryly, remembering how her lover had seized the opportunity to question Dan. Then she gulped. "Dan withheld any remorse. He used his final words to intimidate us until he died."

Pausing for a moment to consider a happier topic, Carrie mentioned, "I think there's a portal for dragon flyers at Acadia National Park."

Joan tuned in remotely to the region and agreed, "I get that too. Let's go there tomorrow for some cross-country skiing."

"And portal spelunking!" Donna added in slight jest. She rose from her place beside Carrie and mischievously dropped the pillow on her friend.

Carrie covered her face quickly and caught the pillow. Donna left the room to go to bed before calling, "Goodnight everybody."

Carrie tossed the pillow lightly at Joan so that she wouldn't feel left out. Joan reached out and caught the pillow in midair with a satisfied smile that she had not lost her quick reflexes. Carrie stood and walked over to the couch. She began arranging sheets and blankets with Joan's help before contentedly snuggling under her carefully sorted pile. Joan wished her goodnight and departed down the hall. Then Carrie turned off the light to the small lamp on the adjacent end table.

The next day the three women drove to Acadia and met Yanni at the ski lodge.

"So we are on a portal hunt!" Yanni said with excitement as he put on his skis outside the building along with the others. He made sure that no one else could overhear him.

"We detected a portal for Dragon flyers," Joan explained. Then she consulted Carrie, "What do you think about going down that trail to the west of the park?"

Carrie nodded. "Let's give it a mile and a half."

Donna and Yanni looked at each other with a wry smile. There would be no wild goose chases with these pragmatic individuals leading the hunt.

After a mile down the trail, the group stopped at the outskirts of a clearing in the forest. They stood outside of the ski tracks and positioned themselves on a bank off the groomed trail so that other skiers could easily pass.

"This is it," Joan announced.

Yanni nodded. Carrie and Donna surveyed the meadow for more information.

"I'm getting that the Dragon flyers existed thousands of years before ancient Egypt and after the fall of Atlantis," Donna told them. "They lived in structures that floated high above the Earth. They tethered the structures to the forest."

"I see it," Yanni and Joan said in chorus, when they adjusted to viewing the scene in other dimensions.

"They were attacked by entities with Reptilian faces for airlifting survivors. The survivors were from a group of people who hid in caves," Donna continued. "You know, the Dragon flyers remind me of Santa Claus."

"Me, too," Joan agreed with a smile.

"The leaders were captured and imprisoned," Donna related. "The rest fled to an island after they killed the elves. This portal is for the survivors of the Santa Dragons."

"Apparently they took the leaders to their base near the North Pole," Joan interjected. "They conducted experiments on them in the use of torture for mind control. The Chief Medical Officer perished before a group made their escape. The woman who was third in command was killed while escaping. The leader and the commanding officer made it back safely and mounted an attack against the Reptilians. However, the leader had plea bargained for his release and the mission failed. Only those who made it to the island survived."

"So this Santa Claus became a traitor," Donna commented.

"I've always wondered about the fixation on toys," Joan mentioned. "It is like a set up for a codependency, though I can relate to the joy of spending time with loved ones over the darkest time of the year."

Several skiers appeared on the trail in the distance. The group on the snowy bank saw them and quickly dispersed. They spilt into two groups and left the trail that they had been on. They met again at the portal twenty minutes later.

"So where were we?" Yanni asked.

"We were talking about Dragon flyers," Donna told him.

"Oh yeah," Carrie remembered, picking up the rest of the story. "The survivors of the Santa Dragons joined with other remaining cultures. They started the tradition that many people today associate with the Camelot myth, only in reality it was much different. The myth was created by those who lived in 700 AD, several hundred years after the original existed. The survivors of the Dragon flyers refer to the civilization as Camelon."

"It was like an Armageddon," Joan interjected. "A major conflict between the planetary forces of good and evil almost resulted in the destruction of the planet. There's a lesson in this portal. Apparently the planet is headed down the same path again. Something needs to be brought back from the past into the very near future. That's why we need to be here."

"I have it!" Yanni shouted. "It's wisdom. What would the Camelon civilization had done differently?"

"Trust no one," Carrie.

"Got it," Yanni murmured.

"There is something else they want us to know," Joan insisted. "It has to do with my namesake."

"Do you mean Joan of Arc?" Yanni questioned.

"Yes, for the sake of clarification," Joan replied. "We are correcting the archetype of the female warrior, while bringing it forward into the future. We need functional archetypes."

"She indirectly restored Salian rule of France," Donna surmised, She had quieted during the discussion. After pausing for a moment, she continued, "These rulers had been a major foe in Camelon. Three of the knights were crucified by the rituals of these dark wizards. She served as a warrior of vision like Julius Caesar and Constantine."

"Or a victim of her own ego," Carrie rejoined.

"It is a question of what is being served," Joan agreed. "France just substituted English occupation for the same rulers who sold them out to the holy roman empire. Constantine made it holy, though he was really a puppet. I can see why the lesson of Camelon is 'Trust No One.' "

"Instead of external visions, the prudent route is to follow one's inner voice for inspiration," Donna reframed, steering the interpretation to a healthier alternative.

"Joan of Arc can inspire us for her skill as a warrior, though she was misguided," Joan added. "The healer balances the warrior."

"If you know where to heal someone, then you also know how to kill them," Donna remarked. "The training enhances the ability to read energy as part of the spiritual cultivation."

The group divided again into two smaller groups and separated to avoid attention. They skied for another hour and met at the lodge in the early afternoon. There were fewer skiers around and they felt comfortable eating and relaxing together before driving back. No one mentioned the portal until the women had assembled in Joan's car. Yanni remained silent and waved them off before he took a different route back to his apartment. He would have loved to talk more about the portal, but he knew that he could catch up with Joan later. For the moment, it was prudent to avoid being followed by Nicholas's associates.

"OK, so if I had been a surviving Dragon flyer in a past life, then contacting these portals is a way to retrieve lost soul fragments," Carrie reasoned. "As I integrate history of the past, I am also integrating parts of myself."

"That makes sense," Joan confirmed. "How do you feel now?"

"Much calmer and more whole," Carrie answered.

Donna looked at Carrie and nodded. Carried did seem more relaxed and present to her.

The trip continued without any further event. Afterwards, they picked up some take-out and dined around the woodstove in Joan's living room.

"Joan," Donna said as she reflected on the new details while eating. "Do you think Nicholas is a member of the Bilderberg Society?"

"What do you mean by Bilderberg?" Joan asked.

"My friend from Germany told me that Bilderberg means 'Photo Mountain' in English, which correlates to Iron Mountain in Ayn Rand"s *Fountainhead*," Donna remarked. "Eli has been investigating a similar group of international power brokers who meet every year to decide the fate of the world."

"I know he went to a meeting every spring to meet with bankers, politicians, monarchs, and corporations from all different regions of the world. He said that no journalists were allowed and they met at different places around the world every year. He asked me to go with him once, but I felt uncomfortable with the secrecy. My reluctance signaled the beginning of the end of the relationship."

Donna asked, "Is Nicholas related to any of the attendees?"

"I think he is related to Isabella-Spain," Joan replied.

"Eli observed some occultists attending the meetings," Donna stated.

"Like dark wizards?" Carrie questioned.

Donna answered, "Members of the Nazis occult society."

"There are our Grays," Joan interjected. "Like the portal with the 17th century knight."

"Carrie told me about that," Donna rejoined, before yawning. "I've had a day and a half today. I'm going to bed."

The next morning, Carrie and Donna left to return to Rhode Island and the cape. Joan called Yanni to fill him in on details and made plans to visit some relatives in New Hampshire. They decided to wait until spring. Travel conditions would be much easier after winter.

Yanni enjoyed visiting Joan's parents, who had retired near the White Mountains. They divided their time between Joan's parents and hiking in the mountains. One afternoon, they came across a gorge with a breathtaking waterfall.

"I'm detecting another portal," Yanni observed after they had spent several minutes gazing at the spectacular view of the waterfall.

"I was just thinking the same myself," Joan replied as she peered at the rocky cliffs on the other side of the bridge.

"This one relates to the Fall of Constantinople."

"Some members of the clergy left a gate open for the Turkish invaders."

"Why? That doesn't make sense."

"It does if you are a Druid convert."

"You mean some of the conquered Druids from Europe made their way into the hierarchy of the church?"

"Yes, that appears to be the case. After the church fell, the Renaissance was ushered in."

"The same sultan and his Turks also defeated Dracula and went on to free the Franciscans in Bosnia."

"Do you mean the same Dracula of Bram Stroker's novel?"

"Yes. His family claimed to be the son of the dragon, which also meant *devil* in those days."

"Like Reptilian?"

"Possibly. I don't want to get into the vampire bit. I never did like those horror movies."

"They were spiritual predators, who sucked the blood from the people they killed in battle."

"They can't create so they predate on the souls of those who can. That's why their demise encouraged the Renaissance."

"The sultan, who freed the Franciscans, acted in the same manner as an ancestor at the time of Francis of Assisi. One of the sultans liked the Franciscans so much that he gave them custody of the Holy Lands.

"Well, you know those Franciscans with their stigmata. They are like walking crucifixes, and you know the effect of a crucifix on a vampire. If I was a sultan, I'd want a few Franciscans around me for protection. Can you just imagine me as a sultan?"

"Did the Ottoman Empire have harems? Yes, I can see you as a sultan teaching all the women how to belly dance with Franciscans. I must have been a Whirling Dervish."

"It's you. We all have got to entertain the troops and come out of the closets sometime. Most of the sultans preferred men and kept their women dancing, Let's stop before I get dizzy."

Despite his lighthearted humor, he had an eerie feeling that they were being tracked by Nicholas and his associates. He didn't want to press their luck.

Joan understood his glance and lead the way back to the main trail. She was ready to plead information overload regardless of Nicholas. Although the color had returned to her cheeks, she needed some time to rest with all this information.

"One other question remains," Joan observed. "If the Franciscans held custody of the Holy Lands since the time of Francis of Assisi, then why were the crusaders sent to conquer the Holy Lands?"

"It is simple, my dear. There is no such thing as a holy war and the authorities of the Holy Roman Empire did not respect the Franciscans. Maybe it had something to do with their desire to live like lilies of the field."

Joan nodded with a half smile. Though she found Yanni's manner amusing, she also could feel the historical weight of his words. She felt unsafe, having realized that Nicholas perpetuated this Holy Roman Empire.

They made it back to Joan's car and left the White Mountains in time for dinner with Joan's folks. The next day they said good-bye to Joan's parents and drove back to Joan's cottage in Maine, where they called Larry with the latest news about the interdimensional portal connecting to Turkey.

"I'll let Donna and Eli know. Donna can contact Carrie with the information. I think Carrie plans to visit her next weekend," Larry told Joan. Then he added, "Say, next summer there's a big international geophysics conference. 1985 will be the 50th anniversary and they will hold it California. Would you like to join me? It is near Big Sur at an Institute there. I hear the place is beautiful."

"Sign me up." Joan laughed as the thought of a romantic getaway appealed to her at the moment. She winked at Yanni, who was obviously eavesdropping the best that he could.

"From Turkey to California," he grinned at her after she hung up the phone. "Sounds like another portal to me."

"You may be right," she said seriously, already feeling pulled to the region. "No rest for the weary. I hoped for a romantic getaway."

"Call it a romantic adventure." Yanni chuckled.

Joan blushed slightly and threw a pillow in Yanni's direction. He caught the pillow and tossed it back at her. She stopped, feeling too fatigued to continue the playful fight. "I give up. Time for bed. I go to work tomorrow."

Yanni came up to her and gave her a big bear hug. "We will get through this and keep our balance," he promised. "I know these are grave times, otherwise these portals would not be so important to activate right now. We are being pulled to a destiny that is shattering our fundamental view of the world."

"Thanks," Joan responded as she softened in his arms and then pulled away so that she could retire for the night.

Yanni wished her goodnight before heading for bed himself. The next morning they went separate ways for the time being. Joan continued working at the hospital and Yanni focused on his research at the institute. They remained in close contact with their friends and prepared the best that they could for the future, which seemed to be unraveling quickly in their lives.

Joan joined Larry for the 1985 conference in California. She took a separate flight to California and he picked her up at the airport in San

Francisco. They stopped at a local health food store and picnicked in the city rose garden. Sprinklers were running in most of the park, so it took them a moment to find a dry patch of grass.

"There's a portal here," Larry said as he munched on his roasted vegetable with hummus sandwich.

"It's a very ancient one," Joan surmised. She rearranged the feta on her pita bread before taking her next bite. "It is pre-Atlantis."

The couple gazed at the surrounding rose bushes and sniffed the aroma in the park.

Larry continued, "It pertains to a Lemurian underground."

"I got involved. The planet underwent programming by a race of aliens, who masqueraded as authority figures. My father tried to impress them. He betrayed me and they executed me. They ran a laser through my abdomen."

Joan quit eating and put her pita sandwich down. She noticed an odd sensation in her stomach and that she had suddenly lost her appetite.

"I had been some sort of priest who observed the political dynamics," Larry conjectured.

"I know,"Joan said, dazed. "They wanted to bring you in for questioning, but we created enough of a distraction so that they had to focus on us.

"Who is 'us'?" Larry asked Joan.

"Me and my cohorts," Joan answered. "Donna attempted to help me escape. I became very saddened by my father's greed. I lost contact with my cohorts and they killed me. Somehow, in spite of the circumstances, I won."

"Well, you have better chances for survival now. You haven't lost connections with your cohorts."

Joan's countenance brightened with this realization. She took a deep breath and allowed more information to come forward. "The Serpentines were infiltrating the population and disguising themselves to look like the others. We saw through their masks."

"Nobody believed you," Larry told her. "Others sold out and complied with the Serpentine agenda."

"Serpentines and their lackeys fed off the Light Beings responsible for cultivating the earth spirit," Joan observed. She sighed and laid down on the grass. Flurries of white clouds were quickly making their way across the sky. "It all happened very fast and nobody fully understood what was going on."

"Except for a few," Larry acknowledged. He leaned over Joan and kissed her.

She closed her eyes and drifted away. She felt as airy as the white clouds overhead and her head began to spin. Larry kissed her again and she allowed him in the deepest recesses of her spirit. Somewhere she found him deep inside and she wrapped her arms around him. Pulling him closer, her fingers moved upwards and fathomed the features on his face. Already soaring from her position pinned underneath Larry, Joan fell into his embrace and allowed him to cradle her in the void. She could sense him in the darkness surrounding her and frantically groped for a connection with him. It was something she had missed long ago and she wanted to find it and hold it forever in her mind. He held her in his arms and kissed her deeper and deeper until she disappeared in the clouds.

"I lost you," he softly said.

Joan could hear him but she didn't respond. She let herself go and fell into a temporary light sleep. Larry released her and turned on his side to lie down on the grass beside her. When she awoke, he helped her to her feet and led her out of the park. She settled in the passenger seat of the car and napped while he drove quietly along the coast towards the lodge. Joan awoke shortly before they reached their destination. After checking into their room, she reclined on the bed and lapsed into a slumber. She heard Larry tell her that he was going to a meeting and would return later in the evening. Then she nodded and waved him off in her half-conscious state.

When he returned, she was ready for him. He took off his shirt and lied down beside her in the dusk. She opened her eyes and ran her fingers across his face. After a brief caress, she kissed him. He returned her kiss and plunged into her. His hands ran across the curvature of her body until she stilled under his spell. He could reach her now and she knew this. Making love through the night, they finally fell asleep in each other's arms when the early morning light peeked through the curtains.

Later in the morning, Larry attended sessions at the conference while Joan swam and took long walks along the beach. In the evenings they dined and went to bed early. They stayed in their own little world and there were few distractions from the conference to interfere from their quality time together. Joan felt more in love than what she had ever been in her life.

They departed for their flights a few days later. When they returned to their lives in separate states, Larry called Joan and invited her to spend next Spring in Ireland with him. He felt she needed to go there to regain her strength on the physical plane. Ever since the California portal she had noticed a weakness in her constitution. Although she still maintained her busy work schedule, it appeared her spirit had been drained out of her.

During the spring of 1986, Joan met Larry at the airport where they boarded a flight for Dublin. They arranged to fly together this time rather than meet at their destination. After they arrived in Dublin, they drove a half hour south to a hotel near Kildare. Kildare in Old Irish translated to 'Church of the Oak' where the ancient Celts had a shrine to Brigid, a goddess that had survived as Saint Bridget in the Christian world. After some rest and a light lunch, they rented bicycles and rode through the country roads. Almost three miles down the road, Joan stopped near a field and got off her bike.

"This is it," she told Larry as he hopped off his bike and stood beside her. "Thank you for showing me this place. This is where I can reconnect with my spirit. It resonates with the place I imagined in the rose garden."

Following her gaze across the hills in the background, he softly whispered in the breeze blowing the hair past her left ear. "You are right."

"It is a portal for the wee people," Joan said with delight. "This is what my soul missed."

Larry gazed at the collection of leprechauns, fairies, and gnomes emerging on the field. The local natives referred to them as the 'wee people,' Larry commented, "The portal connects to a place called the 'Flowery Meadow' near Avalon. They use a communication system similar to the one that Donna has found with the ley lines. It is called the Horsetail Communication Network. These wee people tell us to unravel from the no-win energy system that is bent on the destruction of the planet."

"That's all," Joan decided. "I just needed to know that they were around. I feel better now. It is odd how my energy is related to the energy of the planet, though the connection differs from Carrie's link."

"Yes," Larry observed. "Your color is back and your energy seems stronger. Perhaps the drain relates to the energy vampires like Nicholas and his crowd rather than the direct tap on the earth's spirit. This place sustains the energy for you."

"It is a metaphor for another fork in the road," Joan speculated. "Let's go back to the hotel room," she suggested as she mounted her bike. She had said it plainly without innuendo.

Larry understood her. He silently nodded and lightly put his arm around her for a brief moment. "It is a warning to get back to where we belong and maintain the balance. The energy represented by the wee people transcend the darker reptilian one. I think the balance is a Vedic one. If we seek harmony with the various elements of ourselves, then we become complete with zero energy dependence."

"Let me put in a word for interdependence," Joan interjected. "I never would have pulled through without a hand from my friends." Turning towards Larry, she said, "Thank you for taking me to this spot. You've helped me get my life together in many ways," she told him as she headed back onto the country road.

"I'm making up for lost time," he said before jumping on his bike and following Joan down the road.

At the hotel, they returned the bicycles and went out for dinner.

"I wanted to ask you to marry at the portal, but I didn't have the ring with me," he explained as he knelt beside her and placed a ring on her finger. "Joan, will you please marry me after all these lifetimes. Can we make it official?"

Small tears escaped her eyes before she responded, "Yes."

Then she leaned over him and kissed him passionately while he moved closer in her embrace.

"The truth is that I have always loved you," she admitted. "I have been committed regardless of legalities. We just have to time it so that Nicholas doesn't interfere or destroy the world and our lives with it."

"We have always managed our passions well in the past," he observed as he resumed his place beside Joan at the table. "You are right, we may have to be covert about the committed relationship."

Joan took his hand in hers and told him, "I will wear your ring as a necklace around my neck to deceive Nicholas and his associates."

Chapter Eleven

The glistening gold in the refraction

Of a grain of sand

Builds the steps

To heaven

Tune Reference: *Stairway To Heaven*

----Led Zeppelin

CARRIE MET JOAN at the Bangor train station the week before Thanksgiving. After staying the prior evening with Yanni, Joan appeared fresh and bright when she greeted Carrie at the station. Besides spending time with Joan, Carrie intended to visit an old friend from her home town in Texas.

"You're a sight for sore eyes," Joan said when she saw Carrie. Tears welled in her eyes with the admission. Joan uncomfortably looked down at the ground beneath her feet.

Carrie smiled and embraced Joan. The train whistled in the din and they exchanged small talk. Glancing at the departing train, Carrie lifted her bag to her shoulder. The rest of the exiting passengers scarcely noticed the train's absence.

"There are some more developments," Carrie mentioned once they were away from eavesdroppers. "I heard about it on the train. If you have time, can we go visit the otters at the wildlife refuge?"

"We can grab a bite to eat there. There are some great delis in the area."

When the women arrived at the wildlife center, Carrie went straight to the section where they kept the otters. One of the tanks had a shattered window and was only partially filled with water. In the adjacent tanks, a group of otters were floating on their backs and diving for clam shells. Carrie gazed at the broken window and then studied the behavior of the otters in the other tanks. One of the otters had a bandage wrapped around his left paw.

"The tour guide talked about this refuge on the train as a popular place for tourists. He said that one of the otters had lifted a heavy rock and broke the window. The otter climbed over the broken glass and cut his paw. Then he welcomed himself to a self-guided tour of the refuge center," Carrie explained as she looked intently at the collection of otters.

Joan cocked her head to one side as she listened to the story. She wondered what Carrie was thinking and how it related to their past events.

"Otters don't just break windows," Carrie reasoned. "The otter with the cut hand is trying to tell us something. He is desperate. All the other otters seem frantic, too."

Joan considered Carrie's perspective and turned her attention to the otters in the tank. The mammals did appear stressed for some reason. Their play lacked the usual joy, instead it amounted to worried activity.

"What are you getting at?" Joan questioned. Though she could read merpeople, fairies, leprechauns and understand stress in mammals, tuning into otters was a little bit beyond her capabilities.

"There is something in the water," Carrie said as she gazed at the sea in the distance.

The dark water appeared ominous. Waves danced roughly on the surface. Joan did not see any signs of the merpeople. Satisfied with the information she had gleaned from the otter's tank, Carrie faced Joan and said, "I think that the otters are trying to tell us that there is a national threat invading the inlet. I suspect a Soviet nuclear sub moves below the surface. Energetically, the foreign sub appears on our radar as a nosy, giant mechanical fish that is out of place. This area is stocked with US sub bases. The otters have learned how to ignore them and swim around them. This particular sub appears alien to them. The otters are trying to catch our attention because they sense we can do something about it."

Joan sighed and dropped her shoulders. The idea resonated with her entire body. Suddenly she understood their purpose at the otter tank.

"There is more," Carrie continued. "The cut on the otter's paw is significant. I received a cut on the same hand last week.

"What do you mean 'received'?" Joan queried.

"While I upholstered an antique chair, a nail scraped my left wrist. I am usually pretty well coordinated, but this cut seemed to have come out of the air. My left hand had been traumatized in the past and so any injury to that part of my body causes me to think twice. The cut came really clean. I felt that it had happened for protection."

Joan sighed and turned to face the troubled waters. Everything that she had heard about Carrie from Donna and the merpeople started to make sense, though the revelation startled her. For once she didn't bother to examine a wound. She could feel the depth of the spiritual trauma emanating from a simple cut. Now she could fathom the extent of the otter's distress and understand how Carrie could relate to them, like she had related to the furry dragon in the MidEarth. They were all connected by a past trauma far deeper than the bottom of the sea. Whatever threat existed at the bottom of the inlet had a supernatural component. Joan hated dealing with the supernatural and shook her head.

"Let's go," Carrie said. "I need to get something to eat."

Joan smiled with a nod. Carrie's down-to-earth manner always amused her. The two women left the wildlife center and walked a quarter of a mile to a tiny cafe on the outskirts of town. They found a table inside and sat down to relax before a waitress came for their order.

"Even my cat has been acting unusual," Carrie remarked after the waitress had left with their order. "Time seems to be speeding up. At one point he disappeared in a vortex and I had to call him back. We learned how to manipulate time in second year physics. You know, with Lorenz coordinates and shifting inertial frames. In third year physics, we learned all about tensors and Hamilton transformations with rotating coordinates in more than two dimensions."

Joan shook her head to regain her composure.

"What do you think is happening?" she questioned Carrie. She wistfully gazed at the horizon as if wanting to get to the bottom of things.

Carrie ignored the question. "There's another piece to all this. I met with a hypnotherapist last month, the day after Halloween. The phone rang and interrupted the session in a very profound way. It threw me off. I told her that I had been running from a black dog occult group and she gasped. She seemed to be somewhat familiar with it, though she never explained, except to say that she was trying to get out from under an Egyptian pyramid."

Joan shuddered when she heard about the interference from the occult group. A phone ring would disrupt any induced trance, much more a call arising from an esoteric group known as the black dogs. Both the noise and energy surrounding the call could adversely affect a vulnerable psyche. "It seems to be an occult group associated with ancient Egypt."

"I haven't returned to the hypnotherapist, The session became distorted after the phone call and even the hypnotherapist appeared dumbfounded at the words coming from her mouth. They were insulting."

Joan cocked her head from side to side. She could not believe what she was hearing. Carrie leaned forward and told Joan, "The threat at the bottom of the sea appears to have archetypal proportions."

Joan hung her head as Carrie's words struck a deep nerve within her.

"It's huge," Joan replied, shaking her head again to keep things light.

"There's quantum physics at play here," Carrie observed.

"Not to mention the paranormal," Joan added as she rubbed her head. "Where are you staying?"

"With Brent's relatives south of Bangor. I'm meeting a friend tomorrow at the observatory on the Penabscot River. I have been concerned about her, almost as if I am about to lose her forever. I'm not sure what kind of information I am picking up. I've been really fatigued lately. Time appears to be speeding up while I seem to be slowing down."

"Where can I reach you?" Joan asked.

"Here is the number for Brent's aunt," Carrie replied as she wrote some numbers on a napkin and handed it to Joan.

Joan glanced at the napkin and put it away in her pocket. They finished eating and Joan gave Carrie a ride to the aunt's house. Carrie hopped out the car and waved good-bye to Joan. Joan felt uneasy about the place so she didn't linger. It seemed to spinning in a direction counter to the present velocity of events swirling around them. Years ago, Joan had taken extra physics courses and how to calculate the angular momentum and moment of inertia of objects. She learned the mathematical approach putting a spiral on a football pass. There were equations for the athletic skill, which physicists understood. It was one thing to diagnose an illness in three dimensional space, while it was another to view how a patient's mass rotated with the time dimension. Perhaps the insight into rotational matter came from the lifetime as a Whirling Dervish. Regardless whether they were Whirling Dervishes in the present, Joan realized that Carrie saw the world as a rotational body in space and could easily spot the perturbations. Noticing Joan's discomfort, Carrie nodded her understanding while maintaining her confidence in her own ability to deal with whatever events unfolded. Snug within the coordinates of her present position, Carrie waved Joan away and entered the house alone.

The inhabitants of the house appeared manic in contrast to Carrie's calm. They sensed an ending like wasps at the close of summer and busied themselves without any particular agenda. Long ago, Carrie's mother had taught her to simply roll over and float if she ever found herself in troubled waters. Remembering this swimming lesson, Carrie simply floated the metaphor through the mayhem as Brent and his relations peppered her with taunts similar to those of the aborted hypnotherapy session.

The next day, Carrie went to look for her friend at the observatory on the Penobscot River. However, her friend did not show up. Carrie waited for fifteen minutes and tried all the doors to the building but they were locked. Something seemed off. Not only did her friend fail to show, but she had been given the wrong time to see the facility. Two men who apparently worked there appeared in the parking lot and walked inside a side door. Carrie asked them about her friend, who also worked as a volunteer coordinator at the observatory, but the men yelled at her and denied any knowledge of her friend. Carrie waited outside the facility for a moment. She grew more and more concerned for her friend. She opened the unlocked door and took a few steps inside the narrow lighted hallway. Chills ran up her spine and she turned back and headed for her car. The men emerged from the building and silently walked back and forth across the street on the crosswalk.

"Take your crosswalk," they silently communicated.

Then Carrie knew that she had been set up. The end of the world had come---this stage represented the twilight zone.

Before responding to their overtures, Carrie returned to her truck and for archetypal symbols of inspiration. She donned a corduroy cowboy hat and a beaten-up briefcase that she used for outdoor field work. She knew that her thoughts were being tracked in the collective consciousness and elsewhere. So she decided to give those responsible for this latest Armageddon an earful.

"I have a brief case," she projected, as she played on words with two meanings. "It is called *Play it again, Sam*. My complaint is that I am always arriving to clean things up, like Sam Houston seizing Texas's freedom after the Alamo burned. Here we go again. I need music. *Play it again, Sam*. Events come too fast, like the song by Art Garfunkel, *All I Know Is That I Love You*. This is my case."

Carrie stood in front of the observatory with her briefcase for a moment. Then she placed her inspirational symbols away inside the truck. She crossed the crosswalk and began climbing the numerous stairs on the hill leading to the adjacent city. Midway, she stopped and turned around. She watched the ghouls and dark spirits arrive in the parking lot below her. The distance hid their ugliness, as the crowd gathered for the event. Finding no place left to go but up, Carrie decided against waiting for a final confrontation.

"Cheaters!" she silently communicated to those in the parking lot below. Then she turned on her heels and climbed up the hill, while resuming her train of thought.

"My vote counts," she silently communicated. "All those who want to create their own reality, follow me. This is a bust, you see. The tables are turned on those who attack the planet."

Though the bust resembled the task of walking the plank for pirates, she pushed with her demands. "OK, I need music if I am going to do this."

"First, let's begin with *Crazy For You*, and invoke the madonna archetype in this scene." Carrie waited until the song filled the air around her, then she emphasized some of the words to the song with her thought projects, "...If you read my mind...two by two their bodies become one...throw it together folks," she communicated to those Light Beings who were joining her in her mind. She sensed that she had divine support.

Armed with melody permeating the atmosphere around her, Carrie turned and continued to the hilltop. By the time she reached the top of the hill, she changed her mind about the song. "Cut...cut. OK, it is *Stairway to Heaven*. It is time to bring heaven to earth. This is as good as it gets."

Sure enough, Carrie heard the melody of *Stairway to Heaven* resounding through cheap loudspeakers scattered throughout the marketplace. The cheap loudspeakers made the music sound like melody being piped through an early picture show. The effect proved grounding. She stopped at the entrance to the marketplace. People there had caught on and awakened from their programmed state. Not only had the music been internalized to the loudspeakers, but everyone moved in slow motion as if in a trance. However, she panicked when she saw the shopkeepers closing the stores with her arrival.

"We are in trouble now!" she whispered as she quickly strolled through the marketplace. "Open the shops. Cut the music. This isn't heaven yet!"

The motion of the shopkeepers normalized as Carrie walked around the stores. She carried on and energetically turned on all the fire alarms. Sirens blared and lights flashed when she walked past. Then she left. She hurried down the flights of stairs, hopped in her truck, and drove away.

"All in a day's work," Carrie thought to herself as normal traffic began filling the streets. A car whizzed past her and went in front of her vehicle. *Swimmer* read the license plate.

Carrie returned to the aunt's house but nobody was there. She began to feel dizzy from the effects of the day. Unable to remember her plans for the day underneath the circumstances, she lied down on the bed in the guest bedroom. She wondered where Brent and his relatives had gone.

She rested a few minutes and suddenly the phone rang. She answered it in case Brent tried to contact her.

"Carrie, do you know what you just did!" Joan marveled.

"Yes," Carrie replied. "Let's forget it."

Joan became silent, as she sensed the depth of the event. For once, Carrie did not seem so confident.

"Keep in touch," Joan insisted before she hung up. She didn't press Carrie, who seemed very uncomfortable under the circumstances.

The phone rang again and Carrie answered it. Her mother and sister had traced her to this number. Carrie could not recall whether she had given them this number and told them she was staying with Brent's aunt in Maine for the weekend.

"Do you want to come home? Is everything alright?" they asked.

Carrie felt bewildered by the timing of their questions, but she remained calm and logical. "No, I am fine," she assured them before quickly ending the conversation. She hung up the phone and collapsed on the bed in the guest bedroom. Her whole world seemed to be crashing down on her in a swirl.

Three days later, Carrie awoke and found Brent sitting beside her on the bed.

"You've been out for several days," he told her. Then he began crying, "You are dying. You are leaving me."

The more Brent sobbed, the weaker Carrie became. She felt her body ebbing away. She rose to get some water, but her stomach ached and her low spine burned.

"I must have broken my kundalini," she thought as she hobbled into the kitchen. "It must have had something to do with all that yoga I've been doing recently."

Brent followed her into the kitchen. He seemed different, like another person. "My aunt is returning. She wants to take you to the hospital."

"I had to take the cat to the vet. I found him sick in the closet. We don't know what is wrong," Brent continued.

Carrie grimaced at the thought of her beloved cat lying sick in a closet.

"The brakes in the truck rusted out and I took it to the shop. My aunt can take you to the hospital."

Brent's aunt appeared moments later. Carrie could hear her car backfire before she parked in the driveway. It sounded like several gunshots.

"I've gotta fix that muffler," Brent's aunt almost shrieked as she stepped into the living room.

Carrie noticed that half of her face resembled a monster in a Hollywood horror movie. She raised her left wrist in the air so that the scratch faced the aunt's distorted face. The aunt yelled. The face normalized as Carrie lowered her wrist to the wooden floor.

"We got it,"Carrie said happily.

"How about going to the hospital?" the aunt questioned.

Carrie folded her arms across her chest. Deciding that she wasn't in the mood for anymore horror shows, she allowed them to take her to the hospital. She felt herself getting weaker and weaker. She wouldn't survive long if she stayed.

A few days later, Carrie called Joan from the hospital.

"I told the head psychiatrist where to go in so many words," Carrie told her calmly. "The interns tell me that most women don't like him. He began by playing mind games with me. The interns are going to release me when he goes on vacation in a week."

"I'm so sorry that you had to go through this, Carrie," Joan told her. "I was tracking you, but you got beyond my reach."

"You know, that's the nicest thing that anyone has ever told me." Carrie sighed on the other end.

"Eli checked the records for nuclear sub accidents with the government bureau. A Trident sub collided with the Soviets on the same day that you did the time winkle in the marketplace overlooking the

Penobscot River. They remain vague about the location. They only said it was near the Atlantic."

Carrie sat down on the stool inside the phone booth. She felt her strength beginning to return. "That analytical piece of information grounds me," she said to Joan.

"There's more," Joan continued under the circumstances, as if she had nothing left to lose now. She sensed that Carrie and the planet had already hit rock bottom and beyond. "Yanni brought to my attention that there is a Harmonic Convergence; the planets are in alignment."

"At least some people are celebrating," Carrie said glibly. "We'll figure out the astrological implications later. I blew up the galactic nest for the Serpentine Federation."

"Oh yes, I did see an article in the Science section of the newspaper entitled *Scientists Discover Exploding Blue Super Nova*. They have a picture of it. It does look like a blue snake exploding across the sky. Hmmm."

Joan could tell that Carrie had brightened on the other end of the line, and she felt relieved her friend's spirit was coming back.

"I need to work with the simple life forms from the sea," Carrie said. "We need to work to bring the planet back from another dimension. We gotta start from the very beginning."

"Yanni can set you up with the Institute's touch tank," Joan offered. "Donna is coming to see you tomorrow during visitor's hours. How is Brent?"

"He's different, like he has several different entities or personalities."

"Sounds like he went schizoid after the time wrinkle," Joan conjectured.

"That's something you might recognize better than me," Carrie observed. "I am looking forward to getting out now that I am a little stronger. My latest roommate has red eyes that light up in the night when she sleep walks."

"I almost believe everything now. My intuitive colleagues claim that you took out Lucifer," Joan said.

Chapter Twelve

Parallel truths

Bring people closer

Tune Reference: *Hanging By A Moment*

----Lifehouse

LARRY CAME TO spend the Thanksgiving holidays with Joan, who filled him in on all the latest details. After a quiet feast consisting of take-out food, they sat comfortably around the woodstove and sipped spiced tea. Joan sat close to Larry, who put his arm over her shoulder as she snuggled closer to him. He admired the easy way that she moved towards him as if they had known each other for a long time. Rather than kiss her, he decided to wait and listen. Joan looked up into his eyes and sighed wearily as her head dropped on his extended arm. He did his best to ignore her concerns and ran his fingers through her hair.

"Brent has asked Carrie for a divorce," Joan began, melting slightly under his touch. "His schizophrenia has become apparent, though he refuses treatment. Carrie wants out as simply and easily as possible, so she is pursuing mediation. Her strength seems better than ever, especially since she has been working with the simple life forms in the water tank. Yanni helped her get a position with the institute. She rents an apartment at the same complex and they check up on each other."

"The merpeople applaud her work," Larry commented as Joan softly ran her free hand over his thigh. "Carrie is retrieving the planet from another dimension and slowly bringing it back in an ascended state. I am going to arrange for her to connect with the squids and sea urchins at the labs in Woodsport. For now, the focus is on sponges, starfish, and clams."

"A friend at the observatory in Maine mentioned that they could use some weekend help next spring," Joan added.

"Carrie is bonding the elements. "She is progressing from sea to sky. What else?"

"Donna and Carrie are planning a trip in early summer. There is a geological site near Otter, Montana that they plan to see. Carrie has traced the soul of her cat there. A nearby sheep ranch has promised her a puppy from the next litter of Border Collies. Her cat was euthanized after the time wrinkle. Oddly enough, Carrie's lover at the time, Brent, protected her."

"It is a tenuous process. Don't the Tibetans do that to find the next Dali Lama?"

"They traced the soul of the last one to a boy living in the U.S.. I suppose that you could apply it to pets that help out with time wrinkles."

The next summer, Carrie sent Joan a postcard from Otter, Montana. Joan could feel the strings of light attached to the postcard as she weighed it in her hand. Carrie was weaving a new lifeline for the planet as well as for herself. Joan seized the initiative and began using postcards to rebirth the planet.

"Send me a postcard," Joan told Larry before he attended a west coast conference in the Spring of 1988. "We'll tie the geophysical element to mind games. We are breaking from those internal scrips and creating a new reality. It became so apparent in the time wrinkle. We cannot move forward until Carrie and the infrastructure heals. We must create the new reality before we ascend to it."

Within two weeks, Joan had received a postcard from Larry. There was a picture of a geophysics research ship designed for detecting seismic waves on the card. Joan taped it to her refrigerator beside Carrie's postcard from Otter, Montana.

"I remember doing something like this in Atlantis," Yanni commented when he saw the collection of postcards on the fridge during a weekend stay. "A woman taught me how to tie the energies of the various life forms together like the weaver of a cloth. Remember the Greek Goddesses called the 'Fates'? One of the Greek Goddesses threads life just like you are weaving these links together.

"Nicholas has been at the Wildlife Refuge Center lately," Joan said, changing the subject abruptly. "I think that he has found the time machine in the MidEarth portal."

"Why do you think so?" Yanni asked quietly. The idea of Nicholas at the Wildlife Refuge Center was his worst nightmare.

"I saw a flyer that he was giving a lecture there on whale aggression."

"Is it on how his family treats whales?" Yanni quizzed. He felt indignant about Nicholas' masquerade as a scientific expert, particularly concerning those life forms that his family had hunted for centuries.

"His family operates an international wildlife organization," Joan observed. "It is designated as a nonprofit and the purpose is to raise funds. The organization claims that whales have violent sex."

"Oh, is that why they hunt them down? Those biologists judge all marine mammal sex as aggressive. Who asked them?" Yanni questioned.

"Isn't that like having the fox own the henhouse? I thought he was an economics major, and had gone to Austria to study with the Mises Institute."

"The public overlooks the conflict in interest. I don't know how he made the transition from economics to biology. I think his cousin manages the Federal Reserve. That's also why I think Nicholas and his associates are using the time machine. Maybe that is why Eli's investigation is going nowhere. The strangest things have been happening to thwart it. They seem immune from the courts. Meanwhile, Larry and I have plans to get married in the Caribbean at the end of this summer. We are planning a small covert wedding. Please come."

"So you and Larry are tying the knot right under Nicholas's nose."

"Larry and I figure we were pirates in our past lives. We most likely were privateers looting the British Empire, their opium, tea, and slave trade. Privateers were sanctioned by this continent for several hundred years."

"Apparently you both will be back in your element," Yanni chuckled lightly. "Does that make me first mate?"

"Sorta." Joan smiled. "Nicholas won't think of looking for us there, while everyone holds steady for the time wrinkle. By the way, did you know that Donna is pregnant?"

"No surprise there" Yanni laughed. "I take it that she won't make the wedding in the Caribbean?"

"No, she is still laying low until some of these investigations clear."

"And what about Carrie?" Yanni asked. He been away researching nautical artifacts in the Gulf of Mexico.

"She is holding steady. She is going back to school for her Masters in Physics."

"How's Larry?"

"He has been busy providing geophysical data for Eli's investigation," Joan replied. "I am going to visit him next week. I have a seminar near Boston so I'll rent a car and commute."

The next week, Joan met Larry at the Geophysics building in Woodsport, where she intended to spend some time examining some rocks that they had retrieved from the MidEarth portal. Larry worked in his office while Joan rearranged the mineral samples in a tiny lab next to the reception desk. He had converted the lab into a makeshift darkroom for research. Fascinated by the glow of the mineral samples, Joan turned out the light in the small room to study their appearance underneath a blacklight. Some of mineral samples proved fluorescent and illuminated the dark room.

Before she decided to consult Larry with her findings, she overheard a man confront Larry in his office on the other side of the reception room.

"Drop it there!" the man instructed Larry.

Joan stopped what she was doing to listen more intently. The man's voice reminded her of Nicholas.

"Nicholas! What are you doing!" Larry shouted in a loud, exaggerated voice for everyone to hear. "What is this latest development? You're not advanced enough to be shooting guns. I thought we discussed this at exercise class."

Joan froze with the realization that Larry had raised his voice loud enough so that she would be alerted. The inflection in his voice told her to remain quiet in the closeted lab.

"I want the geophysical data for the investigation on the company," Nicholas demanded with a hint of a hiss.

"Which company? We have quite a few," Larry countered.

Joan knew that Larry stalled for time with his answer. She sensed that Nicholas was holding him at gunpoint.

"The company that your lawyer friend is investigating," Nicholas sneered.

"The one that has been using mind control on its employees so that they could make plastic nukes without their conscious awareness?" Larry inquired.

Nicholas did not respond. Joan heard Larry rise from his chair and surmised that the rest of the conversation had become nonverbal. Suddenly, she felt a draft from underneath the closed door. Someone had stealthily entered the reception area. The eternal soft winds of the cape filled the room, seeping into the closed lab from the floor. Then Joan heard a loud noise from the adjacent room as if someone had dropped a pile of books on the floor. A loud thump could be heard from down the hall. It sounded as if a body had dropped to the ground. Joan listened for a gunshot, but it never came. Instead, the door to the darkroom opened slightly and slivers of gold daylight poured into the room. She saw Donna's face and her round protruding belly appeared in view. Despite being seven months pregnant, she remained light on her feet.

After arriving from lunch, Donna had noticed that something was amiss and slipped undetected inside the front office. She had remained in the reception area away from view and dropped a pile of books to create a distraction. This gave Larry some time to execute the skills that he had been teaching in class. By this point in her training, she and Larry could sense each other's movements like a well-rehearsed orchestra. Donna knew that Larry would seize any opportunity to act. Expecting to meet her friend after lunch, Donna assumed that Joan remained in the vicinity. The purple haze from the closed door of the darkroom provided a clue. Donna immediately sensed that Joan hid there.

"Quit playing with those rocks and get out of here. Go to the Geophysics garage for help," Donna whispered to Joan as she let her out of the darkroom and ushered her outside. She gave her friend a quick hug. "Leave the details to me. Nicholas doesn't know who I am. Larry is fine, but your stalker passed out on the floor. Hurry before he causes more problems."

Accepting Donna's reassuring embrace, Joan maintained her silence. She didn't waste time peering at the scene outside Larry's office She hurried out the door and ran to the garage at the end of the next parking lot.

"There's a gunman in Larry's office," she told the technician there.

The young man raised one eyebrow before he swiftly moved into the side office. He found the number of the State Patrol on the wall and began dialing. Then he looked up at Joan as he waited for a response.

"We've been expecting something like this might happen. Our researchers have been serving as consultants on some hot investigations," he explained. "The administrators instructed us to contact State Patrol first."

Joan heaved a deep breath as she turned towards the gray blue waters of the cape. A few tears escaped her eye and her heart still pounded inside her chest. Refusing to panic, she felt concern for the lives of her friends and how things would turn out. She wondered about Donna, Larry, the future, and whether they would be lost.

Within ten minutes, she and the technician watched the State Patrol cars swarmed the entrance to the Geophysics building. Joan remained at her vantage point, holding the energy for a safe and positive resolution to the conflict. Her instincts told her to trust Donna. For one of the few times in her life, she was not in charge. She had to let go and accept her role. The technician also remained at his station after blocking off the parking lot with extra traffic cones that he found in the garage. He wanted to keep the public away from the scene.

Refusing to waste her time, Joan quizzed him about whether he had seen a tall, swarthy, handsome man approach the Geophysics building.

"He seemed to appear out of nowhere. I only saw him at the entrance to the office," the young man told her. Awestruck, he seemed amazed by his own revelations, being unable to place the man with any vehicle or human form in the parking lot.

Joan astutely studied the young man's expression. She could tell that something about his observations seemed beyond his range of human experience. It continued to puzzled him. Years of training taught her to value the free admissions of her patients, which often led her to the truth.

"Almost like he had appropriated?" Joan ventured, testing the technician to see if he could confirm her worst suspicion. Nicholas had used the time machine to get to Larry and wreck Eli's investigation.

"Yes," he said, eyeing her carefully.

Joan nodded silently and he relaxed his shoulder. "I'm glad that I am not the only one going nuts."

"Call it a shared reality," Joan corrected him. She turned her attention to the scene outside the Geophysics building. Two armed State Patrol officers escorted a tall, swarthy, handsome man to one of the patrol cars.

"Is this the man that you saw appropriate?" Joan asked.

"Yes," the technician confidently said. "It looks like he can appear more easily than he can disappear."

Joan nodded her understanding. The young man had made a point. "Unless he is playing them."

The technician grimaced and resumed watching the scene for further developments. Meanwhile, Joan hid inside the garage so that Nicholas could not see her.

As the State Patrol loaded Nicholas inside their vehicle, an emergency aid car rushed to the Geophysics building with its sirens on full volume. Joan gasped and tried to remain in cool physician mode rather than emotional fiancee mode. At this point in time, she reasoned she would be more useful if she stayed in her head and not her heart.

"Looks like Dr. McClendon was injured. They are carrying him out on a stretcher," the technician related to Joan. Though he noticed she was hiding, he didn't bother to question her actions.Anyone who could get him to admit witnessing an appropriation was not someone he wanted to engage in further conversation. He heard Joan groan before she addressed him again.

"Do you see a pregnant woman?" Joan asked.

"Oh Donna? No, she isn't outside. One State Patrol car is driving away now. She must still be in the building."

Joan peered from outside of the garage a few minutes later. She emerged from her hiding position just in time to see the emergency aid car drive off with Larry. She considered going to the Geophysics building to check on Donna, but realized that the State Patrol might question her as a witness. Deciding to stay clear until she had more information, she considered other options.

"Any idea where the aid car might be taking Larry?" she questioned the technician.

"Probably the local hospital. It's just three miles up the highway to the left."

"OK, that is where I will be. If Donna comes looking for me, let her know that I went to check on Larry," Joan said as she hurriedly walked to her rental car at the other end of the parking lot.

Driving to the small hospital, Joan decidedly entered through the emergency entrance as if she worked there. She found Larry casually sitting up in a gurney a few steps inside the hall. His lower left leg had an ice pack on it.

He brightened when he saw her and raised his arms in a welcoming embrace. She rushed to him and kissed him as tears rolled from her eyes. Their hold on each other seemed to last forever and several hospital staff began to collect around them. Finally, Larry released her and Joan composed herself before they addressed the small crowd around them.

"Oh, don't mind us," one of the attendants grinned. "We were just wondering who this lost hippie scientist belonged to."

The others wearing blue scrubs smiled and nodded. Someone made chart notes.

"This is my fiancee," Larry happily told him. "Talk to her. She speaks your language. She works as a Family Medicine physician in Maine."

The people in blue scrubs immediately turned towards Joan. "We are going to do X-rays. We suspect a fracture on the left fibula."

Joan appeared relieved with the news. She waited to ask Larry about what had happened, hesitating to explain the situation to the hospital staff, who were busily charting for the moment. Instead she planted a voluptuous kiss on Larry's lips for anesthetic effect.

Within days, Larry and Joan were aboard a plane bound for the Caribbean. Rather than resort to crutches, he made his way with a cane for support. Jokingly, Larry told Joan that the cane might come in handy in case Nicholas appeared at their wedding. After the incident at the Geophysics building, they had quickly updated their wedding plans to sooner-rather-than-later. They wanted to seize the moment while Nicholas remained in custody. Keeping their conversation on the plane light, Joan drove them to the resort upon landing.

"You still haven't told me what happened with Nicholas in your office," Joan mentioned as she steered the rental car around the hotel lot. Stopping the car abruptly in front of the valet, she bargained, "Come to my room this evening and we'll make it a date. I'll have a little wine to loosen your tongue. We'll sit on the veranda and watch the ocean waves. It will be a private conversation between the two of us without any eavesdroppers."

Larry remained quiet for a few moments and smiled contentedly with himself, a simple man, who knew how to sidestep machinations without further complicating his life. "OK, its a deal, but you must promise to not cancel the wedding over what I tell you. I do not want to scare you off."

Joan rose out of the car and glanced cautiously at Larry, who grimaced slightly as he maneuvered his injured leg. She watched him hopped out of the car and hand his things to the attendant. For once she did not rush to someone's aid.

"Me, fearless ol' me!" she lightly joked.

"It is not about you. It is about Nicholas and your Achilles heel, oh nature goddess, who is soon to be my wife," he asserted. "It is important for both of us to be alive for the wedding."

Joan frowned slightly with this piece of information. For once it had been safe to be ignorant. "OK, I forgive you. But, only for this moment."

Early that evening, Joan heard a knock on the door to her suite. After peering through the peephole to confirm the identity of her guest, she opened the door and invited Larry inside. He wore a tuxedo and presented Joan with a bouquet of red roses.

"This goes well with the wine I have. Thank you," she said, kissing him affectionately on the cheek.

"You look divine," Larry beamed at her. Joan had put on a strapless silk evening dress with high heels.

"You look dashing. Let's talk," Joan replied as she lightly drew him to her, wrapping her arm gently around him.

She led him to a candlelit table on the veranda. The wind blew the white curtains around the opening and the roll of the soft ocean waves could be heard in the distance. Offering him a chair opposite hers, she helped Larry make himself comfortable around the elegant table. After sitting down, he smiled sweetly and propped his injured leg up on a nearby chair.

"Our topic of conversation," Joan smiled back after making sure that Larry had situated himself.

Within a few seconds her face grew serious. Popping the cork off the bottle, she began pouring red wine into the glasses on the table. Jazz music played lightly in the background from a stereo inside the suite.

"I'm glad that it wasn't a fracture," she began as she handed Larry his glass. Then she raised her glass in a salute. "Here's to the moment."

"To the moment," Larry repeated as he gently rubbed his glass around Joan's until his arm laced hers. He took a sip from his wine glass with his arm interlocked with the woman across from him. Joan followed his move, sipping from her own glass. She closed her eyes as she felt a slight head rush. Both the wine and Larry began to affect her at the same moment. She took another sip while Larry dropped his glass and his hand traversed the contours of her skin. Despite his injury, he managed to move in closer until he nearly kissed her.

Larry began his story in a soft voice, "Nicholas used the time machine to obtain Eli's data. He had a gun on me. When I went to retrieve the disks from the storage room, Donna came back from lunch. She sensed the danger immediately when she walked past the place where Nicholas had appropriated. Donna saw Nicholas with his gun and remained inside the reception area. She knew that I had seen her and created a distraction by throwing a pile of books in the corner. The noise broke Nicholas's concentration and I planted a sidekick to his head when he turned. He went out instantly and did not regain consciousness until the State Patrol had cuffs on him."

Pausing briefly for emphasis, Larry lightly touched Joan's lips as he whispered, "The man is desperate and he would have killed me once he had the disks, which are kept in a safety deposit box. It had been Donna's idea to get the disks out of the office. No one thought that Nicholas was directly associated with Eli's investigation until now."

Drawing closer, he nibbled her tongue before continuing slowly in a low voice, "One other thing. "Nicholas mentioned your name in his semiconscious state. He had not detected the connection between us, though his subconsciousness may be aware of it. Nicholas would have sensed your presence in the dark room once he got past me. Eli, Donna, and I kept the details from you in order to keep you out of Nicholas's radar. These details are emotionally charged and could be used against you. The memories within your limbic system could be used by Nicholas's associates to find you. It may not be coincidence that he was able to use the time machine while you were in the office. He may not be able to track the real disks, but he came too close to you for my comfort. You can see why I waited to explain these details until you were happy rather than distressed."

Joan allowed him to kiss her as she responded between exhales, "Yes, I am happy. Thank you for helping me take care of my limbic system." Then she stopped breathing as a perplexing thought crossed her mind. She questioned Larry, "Why did you think that I might call off the wedding?"

"It is the peril," he answered.

"Oh." Joan sighed before she leaned back and took another sip of wine. "That doesn't bother me. I reason that we are probably safer now than when we were pirating the Roman-British Empire in a past life. The Caribbean is our haunting grounds. This is as good as it gets."

"OK mate, let's order some dinner to go with the wine. Glad to have you onboard, again," Larry announced as he raised his glass in a toast. His arm remained interlocked with Joan's while he brought his wine to his lips and pulled Joan towards him without reinjuring his leg.

Chapter Thirteen

Glaring inconsistencies

Are colder than

*Any truthful confession*s

Tune Reference: *All I Want*

----Toad the Wet Sprocket

AFTER THE WEDDING, Larry and Joan continued to live in separate states with frequent visits to each other. The marriage formalized a preexisting commitment. Larry pressed charges against Nicholas, who managed to skip bail and disappear. Though the lack of protection bothered them greatly, they went on with their lives with greater awareness. For the moment, their conscious attention to detail seemed to deter other attacks. Their network of friends and allies continued to be on the alert for potential appropriations. Meanwhile the scientific community considered how to break or transform the energetic connections with Nicholas and his associates.

"Come visit me in Yellowstone this summer," Larry phoned Joan one evening. "They want me to do some seismic profiling there. Some of the geysers are getting off their scheduled eruptions and they want to check-on what is going on below the surface. They have been having earthquakes lately."

"Sounds very earthy to me. I'd love to." Joan laughed with delight at Larry's proposal.

By the end of August, Joan procured some time for a vacation and met Larry at the airport in Cody, Wyoming. They drove to Yellowstone where they stayed together in one of the lodges.

"Let me show you the site where I've been working," Larry told her as he studied the horizon. He had managed to emerged clean-shaven from his month of camping in the backcountry.

Joan agreed and he veered off the highway to a dirt road. Within the hour, they found themselves in the middle of a steep canyon. Larry parked the jeep in a clearing and they followed the rest of the trail by foot. Joan kissed Larry's cheeks and hugged him when he stopped at the end. There were waterfalls, steaming blue pools of water, red rock, and verdant forests surrounding them. She had never seen so much diverse terrain in one setting.

"There are at least two portals here," she told him as her attention returned to the scenery. "We need to make our own lifelines with the heavens, given the infiltration into the human psyche. We could name it after Donna and Eli's baby, who was named for that famous Light Being who started the clean-up job. You know, bring heaven to earth. Call it the Michael Matrix."

"Let's wait until we bring Donna and Michael along tomorrow," Larry interjected. "The unusual feature is that this terrain matches the time of one of the portals. This piece of land docked on the main continent about the time that the Dragon flyers were imprisoned by the Serpentine Federation. The portal is for those who died in prison," Larry observed. "The earth shifted as a result of the Serpentine's attack. The devastation affected the geological processes severely."

"After the Santa Dragons rescued the children from the Serpentines, they fractured into three separate groups," Joan added. "The top two leaders wanted to experiment on the survivors to determine whether they could adversely affect the consciousness of the Serpentines. The Chief Medical Officer opposed this decision. She later joined forces with a proactive group, who chose to ignore the survivors and mounted a direct attack against the Serpentines. This more aggressive group took orders from the third in command." Joan sat down to maintain her composure, shutting down. Shaking her head at the ground as she steadied her breath, she explained, "None of the options appeal to me."

"If they had kept the child that they had given to the gnomes, then they could have destroyed the Serpentines without harming the child. For some reason, they felt threatened by the presence of this child," Larry said with a sigh. "The two leaders didn't think to use the one with the Serpentine brain implant already in place. The other children died from their implants shortly after obtaining their freedom. While the proactive group was planning their attack, the Serpentines retaliated and captured the entire population. All they had to do was untie the cords that anchored their dirigibles. They tied all the cords together and hauled them into prison."

"The Serpentines had manipulated the communication network of the Santa Dragons. This paralyzed the brains of the Santa Dragons, making them an easy victim," Joan commented after she had recovered. "It reminds me of how a snake sometimes hypnotizes its prey like in the cartoon version of Kipling's *The Jungle Book*. They conducted experiments on the Santa Dragons. This time the group broke into two factions. One group wanted to roll over and accept the experimentation, while the Chief Medical Officer and third in command wanted to fight to the end. The female leaders wanted to fight, whereas the male leaders wanted to submit. Those who joined the fighters were called Radicals."

"The fighters were stigmatized," Larry remarked. "I don't think it is such a radical idea to stand up for yourself."

"I know," Joan agreed with a shrug over the revelation. "The Radicals didn't have much to lose. It is time they cut ties with the Santa Dragons."

"The Chief Medical Officer died while resisting the experimentation," Larry continued. "The third commander escaped but died in another attack. The two nonradical leaders were infused with Serpentine blood and set free by some of the unsuspecting Radicals. Those who freed them did not know about the blood transfusions. The head leader betrayed the location of the Santa Dragons and they were attacked. The Serpentines tried to kill the surviving leaders, but both decided to commit suicide instead. The remaining Santa Dragons beat off the Serpentine's attack and fled further north. They gave up their dirigibles and opted for a more grounded lifestyle, which threw the Serpentines off their trail. After emigrating to northwestern Europe, they formed allies with the Lemurians and Anglos. Together they set up stations for the Dragon flyers."

"Those with the implants and transfusions could have resisted the internal Serpentine influence, but they refused to take control," Joan said, appearing confused by their personal decisions. "There is no dealing with the devil."

"Odd decision, isn't it," Larry commented. "I don't understand their motivation either."

"Yes, I know. It is a sad, hopeless choice. They say apathy is the opposite of love, not hate," Joan added as she lightly hugged Larry around the waist in agreement. "Let's go. I've had enough for today. We can deal with the second portal later."

Larry returned her hug with one arm and together they walked back to the car. The information from the portal had been sobering. They allowed the pristine environment to lift the heavy energy from their shoulders. By the time they reached the lodge, their spirits had been lifted by the grandeur of the natural environment. The couple enjoyed an intimate dinner together and retired early in the evening.

The next day they met Donna in the parking lot outside the lodge.

"How does it feel to be forty pounds lighter?" Joan asked as she greeted and gently hugged her friend, who had a three-month infant tightly wrapped to her in a sling.

Without saying a word, Donna showed Joan the sleeping infant in the carrier. "Michael likes geology, though he falls asleep during seismic surveys."

"With a name like Michael, maybe he's protecting the work crew in his slumber," Joan observed, peering at the content baby. "Do you think that he does any astral projection? I've found a few kids in my practice doing this. The parents could not figure out why their sleep was off. We had to focus on grounding them with homeopathics."

"No, he's grounded like his Mama and Papa," Donna quipped, rearranging the youngster as he squirmed without opening his eyes. "Eli and I are convinced that he is part of the Michael matrix."

"Michael Matrix!" Joan said in a hushed voice. "Larry and I were just talking about setting one up. It is about time. We need to create some protection for ourselves and counter the other network."

"We are bringing the Michael archangel archetype down to earth. It is at a time when the planet needs it the most," Donna stated, lightly patting her sleeping baby reassuringly. "Beats praying. I've learned that God helps those who help themselves. The days of the Bible-thumpers are over; they would be the first tell you that. Even the yogi tradition has a place for divine action. Then there is always dharma, which is different from karma."

Because they had different destinations afterwards, they drove to the site of the second portal in separate cars. Donna was staying with a relative at a neighboring sheep ranch while working part-time with the seismic crew. Eli remained on the east coast to pursue his investigations. They parked at the end of the road as they had done during the previous day. Donna lifted the sleeping infant from his car seat and gently placed him in the sling that she retied around her. She grabbed a backpack loaded with diapers and headed down the trail. Joan and Larry followed holding hands. The couple carried backpacks loaded with supplies and lunch for the three of them.

This time Donna took the left side of the fork in the trail and went in a different direction than Larry and Joan had gone during the previous day. When they approached the site of the second portal, the infant began a soft cry. Donna rocked the child lightly and cooed to it as she studied the environment. The jagged, steep cliffs around her seemed intimidating. The surrounding scene seemed to close in around them. Despite the eerie sense of the place, Donna relaxed and positioned the sling so that she could nurse her baby. Judiciously choosing a rocky ledge, she minimized environmental impact and spread a small blanket on the ground. She took care to avoid disturbing any flora or fauna before she sat down and allowed the infant to suckle her breast under her light T-shirt.

"He's sensitive," Joan commented.

"I know," Donna said dryly. "He wanted to come along. I told him that we were going on a portal hunt and he just burped with a happy smile. Seems to improve his digestion."

The infant briefly stopped nursing and opened his eyes wide. He glanced at the surrounding rocks and took a second or two to smile at the group. Seeming to recognize Larry from previous field trips, he cooed before resuming nursing.

"This portal is on the west end of the canyon," Larry began. "The portal belongs to the survivors of the Santa Dragons, the Radicals who attacked the Serpentines."

Joan sat down on the ledge beside Donna and the nursing infant. "Those who were proactive were able to beat off the Serpentines and recreate their lives. They continued to fight the Serpentines from the new bases that they constructed near the North pole. They redesigned their communication network system and forged new relationships with other civilizations that were seeking refuge on the planet."

Donna propped her infant on her knee so that he could have a better look around and perhaps offer a burp. No sooner than Joan had spoken, the baby burped. Now that her efforts had been rewarded, she allowed the infant to resume nursing. "He's in harmony."

Chapter Fourteen

Playing games
Of masquerade
Takes us further from the
Truth of ourselves

Tune Reference: *This Masquerade*

----Carpenters

JOAN SPENT THE rest of her vacation hiking with Larry and visiting with Donna. Then she returned to Maine and her work. The following weekend, she had dinner at Yanni's apartment and told him about what they had learned from the Yellowstone portals.

"Well, we are getting down to the bottom of it." Yanni grinned as he handed Joan her plate. "I wonder what is next? Nicholas and his associates have been almost too quiet lately."

Joan placed her plate in front of her and reflected briefly on Yanni's words. She took a few sips from her cup of green tea and paused. "I know what is next. Though I don't know where Nicholas is hiding these days."

"Probably busy blocking the courts these days," Yanni quipped. "Justice these days appears regressive. The religious right stacks the courts."

Yanni studied her eyes as he savored his own cup of tea. He nodded for Joan to continue her train of thought. She had a concerned look on her face.

"I am not looking forward to the next swing of the Hegelian pendulum," Joan admitted. "It will create enough chaos to pass Armageddon." She quickly changed the subject, "I came across a portal at the hospital that I was too busy to pursue at the time. I think I can access it remotely and use it to help clean things up."

Yanni smiled brightly at her. "Go for it."

"It is similar to the Garden of Eden, except that the story is a little different from the traditional one," Joan prefaced as she started eating.

"Let me guess, you were the alien that created Adam and Lilith from clay," Yanni said with a light tease. "Your job was to create the human form. We needed one compatible with the environment of the new planet earth."

"It was an experiment," Joan confessed with a slight blush. "All the factions in our galaxy put in their two cents. The Serpentines had the Tree of Knowledge. The Grays did the animal forms. The Blues did the water forms. The Anasazi from the Pleiades stabilized the energy during all the dramatic earth changes. Although the Serpentine Federation had destroyed some of their planets, they still pursued *détente* on this planet. The Lemurians from the Planet Mu coordinated the experiment with everyone's approval. They integrated the results while detaching themselves from the rest because they wanted to remain pure. Even in Atlantis, they refused to mix with the others. After the Serpentines destroyed their planet, they wanted their distance."

"The problem arose between Lilith and Adam when Lilith demanded to be on top," Yanni mentioned with a wry smile. "She had been created as his equal and tried to ruin the entire balance of power."

"Lilith turned it into a dominance issue and Adam responded on that level," Joan explained as she rubbed her hand across her forehead. "What a mess! The lot should have been scrapped then. I cautioned them about bringing animal behavior into the bedroom, but you know the Grays with their dominance games. I asked them to look inwards for spiritual inspiration. It was no use. Lilith left and delivered a child in exile."

Joan quit eating and sipped more of her green tea.

Yanni continued, "So you made Eve from Adam's rib."

"I figured that he might get along better with someone who had been close to his heart. That's all," Joan moaned still rubbing her hands over her head. "It had nothing to do with issues of superiority, which I am sure occurred with the Gray's influence. The Grays must have slipped in an inflated ego or something."

"And the Tree of Knowledge?" Yanni asked, encouraging her to continue. "How about a Freedom Tree or something else?"

"That arrived as a Serpentine plant. It came with a remotely controlled snake and everything. I warned them about that Tree, but they didn't listen. I asked the Lemurians to remove it, but they were afraid to offend the Serpentines, in case they might be provoked into another attack. You know how out of control those Serpentines get. They totally rely on their instincts and it is all fear based. The Tree of Freedom came later. The Pleiadians placed one in Australia and it became know as the Boab. The American Revolutionaries imbided an elm tree with the energy of freedom, designating their own plant 'The Liberty Tree.' "

"Good things take time to figure out," Yanni insisted. He pushed her for information. "What happened in the garden?"

"The remotely controlled snake seduced Eve, who seduced Adam, who denied everything and blamed it all on Eve...They started acting like children. Then they saw how stupid they were and left together. I had nothing to do with it. They were still too intellectually fragile to deal with the Tree of

Knowledge. I wanted to break it to them gently, but they had to try things out for themselves. There was no turning back. The Serpentines had doped that apple with Reptilian DNA that seeded into their brains. For once they felt inferior and it was a shock to their system-like seeing themselves in a mirror, though the image was distorted. People think that the Reptilian brain is the first to develop embryologically, but I suspect that the pineal portion comes first. The pineal gland serves as the spiritual connection the universe and most sensitive to electromagnetic radiation. What a big mistake! People think that we started out as monkeys with snake brains. It's a mess."

"Quit complaining," Yanni told her. Attempting to change the subject before dinner was ruined, he insisted, "The human form got us here."

"Eve wasn't happy with Adam either," Joan lamented. "She fooled him with the apple out of spite. It was like a slap in the face."

"Oh," Yanni said. "You can't have everything."

"But, they had everything," Joan continued. "They still weren't happy and couldn't settle their squabbles amicably. That place was beautiful. Nothing like the world of today. What a mess! And this is how the world started."

"Well, at least it started," Yanni admitted. "Though the Serpentines cloaked it in secrecy."

"Talk about social masks. Then came the Greek gods," Joan moaned. "The Blues played with the human mind and Athens spilled out. The earthlings felt so insecure with their Reptilian brains that they began to hero-worship everything around them. They turned everything into a phallic symbol and some of the Blues really soaked it up. The earthlings began to believe that they came from the sea and developed a consciousness without necessarily a conscience. The mammalian brain evolved as a result. What an imagination! Call it de-evolution."

"Wait a minute there," Yanni interrupted before Joan became agitated past the point of no return. "You're talking about my homeland. I'm Greek."

"Yeah well, some of these earthlings got so full of themselves that they decided to build a huge tower, another phallic symbol. The ancient Greeks erected phalluses too, like the Egyptian obelisk, though maybe, the Egyptians were a little more in balance because they believed in fertility. Fertility is a big issue in a desert environment. These gods or Gauds represented Light Beings who got stuck in egos and could not incarnate on the planet. When their star systems exploded due to war or evolution, they sponsored star seeds, who worshiped them as a way of remembering their origins. Although the Gauds became immortal in this sense, they ceased to live in the true sense. Unfortunately this practice grew egos and the human ego could not get over it. It responded with more potty humor and fixation on the genitals," Joan wailed. "The Grays goaded them on, but it was only another de-evolutionary trick. The earthlings had been instructed to keep their feet on the ground, rather than return to the stars. In the end they all became a babbling bunch of babies and left Babylon. Babble on. Babble on. Big dreams and grand schemes for what purpose? The world became a very lonely place."

"Keep going." Yanni sighed as he threw his hands in the air.

"They had to put ego into everything. Petrified, egofied," Joan ranted. "They carved it in stone. The pharaohs were named after gods and transmitted their energy like puppet rulers. The Norse and Egyptian gods were from a spiral galaxy and their star seeds were known as Centurians. The Aztec gods and South Pacific Island gods were from other star systems."

"Well, you know, boys just wanna have fun," Yanni admitted. "Obviously they wanted to leave their mark on the world."

"For what purpose!" Joan cried as she tossed her hands in the air. "There are so many marks on this world now that we can't find the original, much less ourselves." Then she calmed herself and thought a moment. "There was a sect closely related to the Norse gods called Noris. These were the first Pilgrims on the planet and they divided into two groups. The Noris were humble and survived because they had balanced egos. One group went to the West and the other one went to the East. The eastern group became associated with Tibet and the Buddhist gods."

"I get the point." Yanni sighed. He leaned his head on one arm in resignation.

"So Alexander the Great came and gave it all to the Persians. The Arabs preserved the knowledge of the Greeks before they went out of control. Same information, just a different mask," Joan persisted. "It was the Greeks that taught Alexander."

"My hero." Yanni yawned. "He freed all the misguided Babylonian escapees."

"The surviving Dragon flyers reorganized their lifestyle according to balance. The Tibetans adopted this approach and called it *yin and yang*. Instead of control, they sought self-mastery. This kept their egos in check."

Joan stopped and stared at Yanni. His dry sense of humor finally reached her. She threw her napkin at him in retaliation. Yanni threw his water at her. Joan emptied her glass on his head. Yanni threw his napkin at her. Suddenly they froze in their tracks and began roaring with laughter until tears rolled down their faces.

"What I like about you the most," Yanni gasped between chuckles, "is that you don't take yourself so seriously."

Joan laughed, hugging and kissing him affectionately on the cheek. He held her in a light embrace and nosed her forehead.

"This planet only reflects the state of the universe that created it," Joan admitted as she closed her eyes, allowing herself to relax in his arms. "Originally it was created as a neutral zone for those diverse factions that agreed to live in harmony. Nobody is perfect nor was it ever intended to be that way," she told him. "There are no rules left to break. We are lost."

"Good, then I am glad to be with someone who is so creative," he told her.

"We'll make it up as we go along," she promised.

"And leave the uncreatives in the dust?" he speculated.

"Dust is all that is left of them," Joan thoughtfully replied. "They won't be able to reassemble."

"Let's get dessert," Yanni proposed. "I am up for more."

"There were five elements involved in creating the Earth, just like the Five Element Theory in Oriental Medicine," Joan continued, sitting down on the couch to compose herself. "These were established by the time of Atlantis, which was a melting pot representing the New Universal Order. The Atlanteans brought in the Water Element. The Lemurians provided the Wood Element. The humans along with the earth spirits were responsible for the Earth Element. The Serpentine Federation represented the Fire Element. The Anasazi gave the Metal Element."

Yanni prepared dessert while Joan remained seated. He continued coaxing her, "Then what?"

"The Serpentines tried to gain control over Earth," Joan explained, while becoming dazed by the whirlpool of ensuing events and emotions. "They ran secret experiments on the Water and Earth Elements. The Serpentines disguised themselves, though a handful of Lemurians and Anasazi saw through their masks. When Atlantis collapsed, the masks came off."

Yanni returned from the kitchen area and handed Joan a plate of apple cobbler.

"It is like that now," Joan remarked as she began eating her cobbler. "The Serpentines have masked themselves so that they can carry out their agenda undetected. Even the Grays and Blues are disguised."

"That is why authenticity is important in relationships now," Yanni mused as he finished his cobbler. "Otherwise we'd get lost in this masquerade. All of us, except Michael have advanced degrees. The younger crowd used education as an escape; some went beyond the given information, while their older brothers and sisters stayed on the edge. It takes a scholar, though we are not the type to pursue knowledge for the sake of knowledge, much less for the sake of keeping it all a secret."

"Good thing we are educated. The things we learn in college, like how to unmask the truth," Joan reflected. "That is why this information in the portals is so important. We don't have time for the truth to come out on its own. Carrie's time wrinkle showed us the truth about the state of the planet."

Chapter Fifteen

We began as golden starlight

A Divine child

Trying to get back to the garden

Rather than a dusty warrior

Returning to the devil's ashes

Tune Reference: *Woodstock*

----Crosby, Stills, and Nash

AFTER DINNER AT Yanni's, Joan phoned Larry and told him about the portal at the hospital.

"We always knew you were a nature goddess," Larry reminded her in a light jest.

Joan blushed. Alone in her room, she sighed with relief that no one could see her. She grimaced with determination to become accustomed to having another living being in her space on a day-to-day basis.

"We gotta get back to the garden."

"How?" Joan questioned with a hint of despair.

"I sense there is another portal," he replied. "Let's go to the Big Bend area during the winter holidays. We can do some camping in the desert. The geology is great there and we can do some gridding for geopathic stress."

Joan agreed and obtained some time off from work after Christmas. She journeyed with Larry to the Big Bend dessert. After their plane landed in El Paso, they rented a jeep and drove to the National Park. They set up a tent and camped near one of the canyons in the area. In the morning they went on a guided tour with a park ranger, who showed them the places inhabited by the people that the ranger dubbed the *Cave Dwellers*. In one of the caverns, they examined a stone table that had been laminated by layers and layers of animal fat from food preparation.

"It took thousands of years to get a build up as solid as this," the ranger commented as the tour group ran their fingers across the finish.

"This is the portal," Joan whispered in Larry's ear as the rest of the group dispersed. "Let's stay after everyone leaves."

"The Anasazi lived here," Larry began after they were alone in the shallow cavern. "The portal places them in time after Eden and before Noah's flood, which served to purge the human form and patterning. Atlantis was created during the flood. The Anasazi have been on this planet for a long time. It appears that they even used alternative energy like passive solar and geothermal."

"The Anasazi tell us that the past is the key to the future. They also used the Horsetail Communication Network," Joan explained. She sat down on a nearby boulder to rest as she contemplated their story. "In the past they stabilized the planet during severe changes, maybe that is what we should be doing now."

Larry walked around the cavern like he owned the place. "I am all for planetary stability. The Anasazi were the civilization that ascended after living the pure life. They are returning to the planet from another dimension. It is like they are waking up to move us forward into the future. They inhabited the planet at the same time as the Dogans of northwest Africa and the Aborigines of Australian. All three civilizations have the same physical features and attitudes. They were refugees from the Pleiades. The Anasazi were invited to this planet to hold the energy after the Serpentine Federation directly attacked the Santa Dragons. It signified the breakup of Gondwanaland."

"The Anasazi are associated with the Metal Element because they brought in the Bronze Age," Joan fathomed. The wind shifted and a flurry of debris swirled inside the cavern. She felt a shiver up her spine. "It is time for us to go and leave the garden for the desert. No time for Eden."

Larry nodded. He took her hand and helped her to her feet. Together they left the cavern and hurried down the trail. They followed the switchbacks to a small hill covered with sagebrush and prickly pear cactus. Stopping at the top, they took several deep breaths and looked around the scene.

"It's Nicholas and his associates," Larry said. "He is either here physically or else he is remotely tracking us. Eli warned me that Nicholas might come looking for us here."

"The sagebrush is throwing him off. It is like the Native American ritual of smudging to ward off negativity and gain clarity. The flower essence is for getting out of unwinnable situations," Joan reasoned. "We can stay here and set the energy of the aroma before going back to move our campsite."

"Let's stay in the lodge in the heart of the Chisos Mountains," Larry suggested. "Chisos is Spanish for *spirits*. It is off-season and something should be available. For some reason, I don't think that he will be able to detect us there. The mountains filter out particular frequencies of radio waves."

"C'mon," Joan said a few seconds later as she almost slid down the hillside. "We can remotely discuss the portal as we drive to the mountains."

"Great idea," Larry said as he surfed the loose gravel and dirt behind her.

They quickly loaded the rental vehicle and sped down the highway. Larry slowed for deer crossing the road in the distance. He casted a knowing glance at Joan.

"It is a totem," Joan observed. "The Native Americans have their own version of Jungian synchronicity. They call it *Animal Speak*. The appearance of this deer has a sacred timing in our lives. It is a lesson about rapid changes and flexibility. Like a deer, we need to be sensitive to predators and stay nimble."

"Sounds about right to me. We are on the right track in leaving the desert for the mountains," Larry agreed. "Let's go recreate our destinies."

He drove up the narrow switchbacks to the top of the mountain basin. Then they checked into the lodge. There were several suites available in the off season. After settling in their room, they decided to go for a quick three-mile hike to the rim. However, a thick cloud covered the top of the mountain and severely limited visibility. Instead of venturing into unknown territory under the circumstances, they opted for a short hike around the perimeter of the ranger station. The trail bordered on the edge of a cliff. At one point during the hike, Joan stopped abruptly.

"I am picking up two distinct life forms. One has to do with the presence of positive aliens and the other is human. Someone killed a human being on this spot, and the man left the earth plane in anger."

"You can see the shadows of the aliens in the cloud cover," Larry remarked as he pointed her attention to a whiter shade of pale within the gray clouds.

Joan blinked as she looked in his direction. She could make out their forms. There were many of them surrounding the mountain top. Bearing a distinct sense of contented peace and clarity, they told her with an uncertainty less than one percent that she had arrived. For a moment, she could relativistically determine her position in time and space. Though she may not have been able to determine her speed or motion, it didn't matter.

"You are also picking up on the energy of three intelligence agents that were executed on this trail," Larry said, interrupting her thoughts. "They were disguised as tourists. They were executed by the same international group that Eli is investigating."

"The mist is being created by our helpers behind the veil. Our energy can't be tracked through the thick water vapor. It is helping throw Nicholas off," Joan surmised. "It is like wading through a stream of water to avoid leaving any footprints in the dirt."

"Nicholas's international group has been involved with the negative UFO activity on the mountain," Larry concluded. "There's a spiritual war going between the positive and negative aliens right here. The intelligence agents were sabotaging the group's efforts to provide aid to the negative aliens."

"The intelligence agent insists that every US president since Washington has been aware of the alien presence."

"Well, that might explain why some global initiatives seem to be from outer space," Joan quipped.

Larry eyed her with a grin. "Like out of touch with earth plane reality."

"Yes," Joan replied without a blink of an eye. "The nuclear arms buildup is more than enough to destroy this planet. They must be intending to explode the entire galaxy."

"That wouldn't work for those who came here as refugees," Larry observed.

"That's right. We have to work it out here. Let's head back to the lodge. This cloud cover has an eerie feel about it. I want to contact Donna and Carrie. They may have some insight. I need to talk to them about this."

Larry nodded and they headed back to the lodge for a restful sleep. They left early the next morning and departed for the east coast. If it took a cloud cover to disguise their presence in an area where even intelligence agents were easily murdered, they did not want to linger. Instead, they made the most of their experience on the mountain, leaving before they could be energetically tracked. Their energy fields would be easily polarized in the context of the spiritual war where good and evil faced each other.

Joan returned to her cottage in Maine several days early. Larry remained in the cape to pursue this new angle with Eli's investigation. Meanwhile, Joan made plans to consult with Carrie on this aspect of the time wrinkle. She invited Carrie over for some cross country skiing and to spend the night. Joan spoke with Donna briefly on the phone. She needed to finish a geophysical survey before joining them. In addition, Nicholas launched a terrorist operation in the local school district, and she needed to maintain vigilance with other parents in the area. Meanwhile Eli continued the negotiations with French Intelligence and the investigation into the hazardous waste company.

Two days later Carrie knocked on her cottage door. Joan ushered her in the cozy living room. Carrie entered the room and quickly got down to business.

"Let's snowshoe to the dock to talk," she offered. "They can't track us if we are over water, even if it is frozen."

Joan complied and dressed as warmly as possible. She and Carrie trudged through the snow in the late afternoon dusk. They carefully boarded the dock and took several steps towards the inlet. The water around them was iced over. They didn't dare test its thickness and remained standing on platform.

"On the other side of the time wrinkle, I contacted the positive aliens," Carrie began. "Earth is a big experiment and they needed information. Using Donna's code of numbers, I told them that we had gone past the point of no return here. We had to reverse the time sequence until the ultimate dividing point had been reached. Some things are going to shake loose from the planet to relieve its burden. The rest of the galaxy would suffer tremendously if the earth was destroyed."

Joan wrapped herself more securely in her jacket to shake off a chill. Carrie seemed oblivious to the frosty air and remained in a state of wonder as she surveyed the winter wonderland around them.

"Shortly before Atlantis fell," she continued, "The Dragon flyers were to sent several corners of the planet to stabilize the energy during the Great Cataclysm. They were from Pleiades like the Anasazi. There are seven or eight stars in the cluster and the inhabitants differ from each other. Other Pleiadians were sent to the highest places of the world to work as healers and help those fleeing the global catastrophe. They inhabited the mountains such as those near present day Tibet. There were five groups. One went to northwestern Europe and another went to Siberia. Two groups were divided between southern and eastern Africa. The fifth group passed to the MidEarth, where they stayed underground and served as guardians. The dragons that were sent to Africa were imposters. When Atlantis collapsed, their masks came off. Most proved to be giant lizards, Komodo Dragons, and they ate their riders. They were the guardians for the Serpentine Federation. The authentic furry dragons escaped with their riders to places like Easter Island. The two groups lived in the skies over the rapidly changing earth. They tethered their homes, which floated like dirigibles to the planet with cords. The forests grew underneath them as the water receded and Earth settled."

Joan started to noticeably shiver and Carrie turned her attention to her.

"Let's get you back in before you get hypothermia. You were a little out of it to begin with," Carrie said as she helped Joan to her feet. She had been sitting on a nearby bench and could not seem to get warm.

Back at the cottage, Joan warmed in front of the wood stove as Carrie prepared some ginger tea. Handing her the steaming hot brew, she noticed the quiver in Joan's hands, and fathomed her fragility. For the moment, their discussion ceased until they both had been refreshed by a restful night's sleep.

Chapter Sixteen

Turning a shattered existence around

Can get to be a positive habit

Given the need for change

Tune Reference: *Shattered*

----O.A.R.

"I NEEDED TO this thing around," Carrie explained to Joan during breakfast the next morning. "The past is the key to the future. After the time wrinkle, the planet we realigned the planet according to the Five Elements of the Native Americans who learned from the Anasazi before they ascended. Instead of using the Five Elements of Atlantis and Oriental Medicine, I changed the point of reference to the indigenous people. It is a different inertial frame than the Atlantean one. Gods such as Pele and the volcanoes provided the Fire Element. The plant spirits became known as the Wood Element. The Lemurians and Anasazi pertain to the Wind or Air Element. The water spirits are the Water Element. The humans and minerals belong to the Earth Element. Gridding in this inertial frame will stabilize the planet."

Joan sipped her cup of ginger tea and silently stared outside at the flurry of snow swirling in the hazy morning air around the cottage. "So you have outside help."

"Yes," Carrie answered. She quieted, waiting for Joan's response.

"We need to talk to Donna about all this," Joan suggested.

"Yes, I know. I think that she is coming up in two weeks. She and Eli want to celebrate Thanksgiving in Maine. We can get together then."

Later in the month, Donna joined Joan and Carrie at the cottage. They huddled around Joan's wood stove with cups of apple cider.

"You mentioned that you wanted to discuss more intricacies of the time wrinkle," Donna began as she stretched in front of the fire in the wood stove. Eli watched the baby for the evening, and she relished the chance to relax with her childless women friends.

"Carrie is using Native American elements for the virtual reality planet earth," Joan explained.

"That makes sense. We picked it up on our end," Donna commented in a casual tone. "I have a group of mothers and pre-toddlers. We meet every other week to do planetary grid work with our infants. We call ourselves the Force of the Foursome. Sometimes we have as many as six join us on our field trips. Then we change our name to the Force of the Sixsome."

Joan and Carrie chuckled at the thought of a pre-toddler group incorporating metaphysical work into their child play.

"Don't laugh." Donna grinned. "We take ourselves seriously. I could tell that the Native American element posed significance. All the mothers signed up for Tipi Trek next spring. We get to sleep in tipis and dance with the Native Americans."

"That's reassuring," Carrie told her as she relaxed on the sofa. "From here I can see Joan's collection of postcards on the fridge. There's even one from the Four Corners of New Mexico, Colorado, Arizona, and Utah. It is a picture of Mesa Verde where the Ancestral Pueblo Indians lived in the cliffs. Didn't the Navajo call them the Anasazi?"

"Yes," Joan rejoined. "There's a link."

"We are all doing something to stabilize the energy of the change from one inertial frame to the next," Donna said.

Quickly redirecting the focus, Joan interrupted them, "OK, there's more information coming. Where is our next portal?"

"The swimming pool at Yanni's apartment complex," Carrie proposed.

Joan smiled in delight at the immediate response. She took a moment to breathe and then continued, "Can we access it remotely?"

"Probably, I've put in enough laps there. There's energy in the pool," Carrie quipped. She had rented an apartment near Yanni before moving away to pursue graduate studies in physics.

Joan tried to maintain a serious face, while negotiating Carrie's dry sense of humor. She stared at Carrie, who had been gifted with a comic sense of timing as well as a cosmic one.

"It is about some rings that several Turkish wizards forged after Constantinople fell," Donna interjected, before Joan burst into laughter and lost the thread of their discussion. "At the time, people were infusing energy into objects, sorta like Excalibur. Those who possessed the rings served as the guardians of the virtue. There were five rings symbolizing Love, Power, Light, Truth, and Hope. A duplicate was made of the Love ring because no one completely trusted that particular wizard."

"All's fair in love and war," Carrie observed. "The Power ring had the strength of three atomic bombs in it. The guardian destroyed it because people wanted to steal it. They would have used the ring's power for the wrong purposes."

"Love is Power," Joan said softly. She turned and spoke to Carrie directly. "You used the energy of the Power virtue to counteract the nuclear mishap in the time wrinkle---an Aikido move."

"I know," Carrie answered quietly as she looked up at the ceiling. "My ex-friend, who set me up could not be trusted. I won the Love virtue too. The energy of the original Love ring has been deactivated."

"It is a slippery slope that we are on," Donna remarked, putting things in more grounded terms.

"Eli is the guardian of the Hope ring," Carrie continued.

"Little does he know," Donna added. "We should tell him someday."

Carrie could not help but chuckle.

"I bet that Larry has the Truth virtue," Joan conjectured, before Carrie's mirth distracted them. Maintaining her serious tone, she remarked, "It seems to help protect him from Nicholas and his associates."

Carrie shrugged and nodded affirmatively.

"Who has the Light virtue?" Donna questioned.

Carrie cast a glance in Joan's direction. Joan blushed and hung her head as she stared at the floor.

"Oh well," she said with some chagrin. "I can see why we all came together on this project."

"So you get to hold the torch," Donna said as she sunk back into the sofa and relaxed.

"Now what?" Joan asked quizzically.

"We play it by ear," Carrie answered.

"Like improvise?" Donna asked. She turned and rested her head on Carrie's leg as she propped her feet over the edge of the sofa.

"It could be worse," Carrie commented.

Joan threw up her hands and went to the kitchen for snacks. "Wait until I tell Yanni. He is really going to love this one."

"He can make his own ring," Carrie said flippantly.

"He would." Joan chuckled.

"I know." Carrie, who always seemed to be half serious, smiled at Joan. "See what he comes up with. If we like it, then he can keep it."

"It may take awhile," Joan observed with a sigh. Technology was much different a thousand years ago.

"There's more," Carrie interjected, rising to her feet and leaving Donna stranded without a pillow. "During the time wrinkle, another pattern was added to the planetary grid of energy. I also had outside help with this. We connected to Enchanted Rock, a batholith made of pink granite in the heart of Texas. There were four other points of reference. They include the red sandstone formation in Australia called Ayers Rock and Plymouth Rock in Massachusetts. Plymouth Rock is granite boulder that was deposited by a glacier. The third point was at Easter Island, which is surrounded by three crater volcanoes. The ancients referred to it as the Center or Navel of the World or Eyes Looking at Heaven. Easter Island serves as an important geodetic marker. It matches the transcendental set that Joan and Larry practice. The abdominal area is the center of inertia for the human form. The center of inertia is important in the rotation of objects in three dimensional space, such as the planet earth."

Joan listened attentively to Carrie's explanation. She returned from the kitchen with some light snacks. After placing the tray on a coffee table, Joan relaxed in a soft chair and gazed at the fire burning in the wood stove. "There's one more major connection on the time wrinkle grid. This one relates to the inspiration for James Hiltons's *Lost Horizons*. He found his vision of Shangri La while hiking around Ashland, Oregon. The area is the home of the Oregon Shakespeare Festival. I went there with a friend one summer."

Carrie smiled and agreed with Joan. "The fifth point is Pilot Rock near Mount Ashland. The monolith connects to Easter Island on a ley line from the Oregon vortex. It lies in the foothills of the Blue Mountains and serves as a portal to Shambhala, where the healers went before the Great Cataclysm."

Donna picked up the trail of their discussion. "The indigenous people helped you with the time wrinkle."

"Yes, they picked up on it," Carrie agreed. "But, not all are transitioning."

"Like the headhunters in Africa that are regressed Serpentines," Donna continued. "Then there are wandering lost tribes in Siberia that are descendants of the surviving Arctos, the ones who lived in ice caves. They never made it to Tibet to heal and they are stuck in the trauma."

"The people that operated places like Stonehenge had a custom. Every generation added to the energy network. The time wrinkle is the addition to the system. The indigenous people help move the time wrinkle forward and stabilize the planet. The theme pertains to the dream world because it was birthed out of a conflict in a psychic war between good and evil. These five major places represent zones where people go in their higher visions and dreams. This generations' gift to the Stonehenge network can be encapsulated in one word, *vision*."

"We must imagine a better place before we get there, regardless whether it is by necessity or choice," Joan summarized.

"It is the clear day vision that you told me about many years ago," Donna told Carrie. "MLK had his *I Had a Dream* speech. JFK had a vision for the New Frontier. Nobody promised a rose garden, but they dreamed about the possibilities. Enemies shattered it, like the Garden of Eden."

Joan glanced curiously at Carrie, who stared reflectively into space and nodded her head.

Chapter Seventeen

Information from primary sources

Always beats gossip, speculation, and innuendo

Especially in a relationship

Tune Reference: *'Til I Hear It From You*

----Gin Blossoms

FOR THE WINTER holidays, Joan and Larry stayed with Donna and Eli at their little bungalow by the waterfall. They cleaned up a few portals in the area during a short hike. Afterwards, Joan and Donna lingered in front of the waterfall and quietly allowed their thoughts to drop through the swift moving currents. Many events had passed since the wedding and discovery of the MidEarth portal.

"There's been no sign of Nicholas and his associates so far," Eli observed as they relaxed at the table after dinner. "We must be eluding them with our portals. Unfortunately, the investigation is still mired in bureaucratic red tape."

"It could be worse," Donna said as she lightly patted his thigh in reassurance. "It's just a matter of time before its over. We'll keep clearing Nicholas's portals and cleaning them up."

Eli quieted in thought for a moment. Then he changed the subject, "Tell us about the Pilgrims?"

"The ones at Plymouth?" Donna questioned.

"No, the ones that you told me about at Plymouth," he reminded her. "The ones that came to planet earth on a platform after the breakup of Gondwanaland."

Joan, who had been lightly dozing with her head resting on her hand, suddenly perked up. She dropped her hand to the table and glanced at Donna.

"Well, alright," Donna agreed. "Now that Joan is awake, I suppose I will have to tap into that portal. It is beside the waterfall where we got married."

"Lay it on us," Joan encouraged. She sat upright in her chair and refilled her cup of green tea.

"Many thought that they were thieves, but they were really intergalactic refugees. The Serpentine Federation had blown up their planet. They agreed to come to earth to teach in exchange for a planetary residence. They arrived shortly before the collapse of Atlantis. The three people responsible for the Great Cataclysm made a deal with these refugees, who validated the rebel's concerns about the Serpentines. They arrived in Atlantis and left with the Dragon flyers to northwestern Europe. Because of their former experience with the Serpentines, they didn't trust the leadership of the Dragon flyers. They sensed that some of the Dragon flyers would try to compromise with the Serpentines in the end. These star seeds were from Noris and after the waters receded, they lived on the ground. They built sod houses in the meadows. People came to join them and learn. They made occasional visits with the Bear people, or Arctos, near present-day Siberia, while limiting their contact with the Santa Dragons residing over the adjacent forests."

Larry added a few more details to Donna's story as the rest listened. "Almost half of the Noris settled in the east with the healers in the high caves. Many arrived on the planet with severe spiritual wounds from the war with the Serpentine Federation. The Noris understood that balance was critical to spiritual survival and promoted this, which is one reason that they kept their distance from the Dragon flyers in northwestern Europe. They sought Vedic balance with various elements. The Noris wanted to literally keep their feet on the ground as a reality check. It paid off in the end. They burned peat for fuel and used wind power. Merlin's teacher came from this group of star seeds."

Joan followed the course of discussion in her semi-sleep state.She had been spending long hours at work and was feeling the effects during the winter holiday break. As a result, she opted for the big map in her personal life so that she wouldn't overwhelmed herself with details. This allowed her to regenerate at a leisurely pace, while remaining alert for anything that seemed out of place.

"There's more to the story of the three rebels that sunk Atlantis," Joan sensed.

"I can pick it up," Eli interjected. "The Atlanteans considered them comedians. They consisted of two men and a woman. Their names were Moe, Curly, and Lari, which was short for Curly's girlfriend Lariece. Being androgynous, Moe didn't want to get emotionally involved in any relationship and sought balance in his life. The lovers played off Moe, the single man from the Noris star-seed. Moe was a veteran of the Serpentine's attack on his former planet, which they succeeded in destroying shortly after he escaped with the others. Having lost his girlfriend and many best friends in the trauma, he remained wounded from the experience. He had severe survivor's guilt and didn't know how to fit in. Curly and Lari undertook the challenge to entertain and amuse Moe."

"Moe's trauma sensitized him to the actions of the Serpentines and he saw through their masks," Larry continued. "Curly and Lari enjoyed pulling Moe out of his isolation. Moe thrived on the humorous interruptions to his one-man comedy routines. They were gentle and valued his perspective, which matched their deepest suspicions about the Serpentine's subterfuge in Atlantis. Although the Atlanteans greatly respected their abilities as scientists, they also saw them as one big joke."

Joan shook her head in chagrin. "Like any other wounded healer, I can understand both sides. You must---to be able to heal."

Larry turned to her with a huge grin and admitted, "I know she's not androgynous. Like any other artist or healer, she maintains a balanced perspective."

Donna laughed. "Don't shoot the messenger. Give me a break. So I am passionate about my work. I just don't get caught in my own mirror. I remain objective. There's another Greek god for discussion. I think they named him Narcissus."

"You know how I like people who love their work," Larry interjected as devil's advocate. With a hint of innuendo, he put his arm around Joan. "I swoon over maps, too."

Joan blushed slightly with his embrace. She decided to redirect the course of discussion before things went too far, "Alright, let's get back to the story."

"No," Eli protested. His legal mind loved a great debate. He proposed another argument, "This is an important lesson from this portal. It is about context and content."

"That is one of Carrie's favorite topics, except she defines it in metaphysical terms," Donna quipped. Instead of arguing with Eli, she threw him off his position with her wit.

"Alright, let's get physical," Joan said as she dug in her position. "The vagina is the perfect example of context and content. Sometimes it serves as a portal for delivering babies, and other times ..."

"Let's censor those other times," Larry added as he patted Joan on her abdomen. "We are pregnant. We wanted to wait until we had sorted out the details of the short-distance relationship, but since the topic came up, I thought that I'd use it to support my argument."

"See what I mean about space for rent," Joan explained to Donna and Eli, who were dumbstruck with the news.

"Michael is going to have a little playmate," Donna announced, lovingly glancing at Eli. Almost one year old, Michael had fallen asleep after dinner and rested contentedly in a nearby room.

"The baby beat the contraceptive odds," Joan admitted, still in emotional shock from the revelation.

"Meant to be," Donna stated simply. "They are called surprises."

"The wounded healer is allowing us all into her life," Larry said as he rubbed Joan's shoulder. "Just think of it as an opportunity to play out the Chiron archetype. Your patients will benefit from your understanding as a mother."

Eli wisely ended the intense discussion. He raised his cup of chai and began a toast, "Here is to intimate friends. We all need each other."

Those at the table appreciated his remarks. The group happily smiled as they joined his toast.

"Cheers," everyone softly echoed as their cups clanked together.

Joan remained speechless for the moment.

Larry lightheartedly steered the conversation back to the information pertaining to the waterfall portal. "There is more information from the portal. It has to do with the gods of the South Pacific Islands and resulting breakup of Gondwanaland."

"Researchers are convinced that Oceanic mythology is closest to the Jungian archetypes," Eli commented. "Archetypes as structural elements of the human psyche, seem to be the purest in this part of the world, despite years of continued migration in the regions. There are many similar myths among the Islanders. This gave them a common ground for understanding as they traveled from one island to another."

"Yes, but they don't make a solid foundation for the human psyche," Joan insisted. "Remember, the gods were unable to make it as human beings due to their egos. They continued to torment the star seeds from afar long after their demise. Myths developed after the unmasked Serpentines mingled with the star seeds. The myths reflect this traumatic history of deception, dog-eat-dog worlds, sun gods, and island births. Though they may have been in the consciousness, the myths didn't necessarily support communities. Sometimes they served as a reference point for further violence and destruction. It gets as messy as the interactions stemming from the Garden of Eden. Solar power is not the same as sun worship. Instead, we could call it solar empowerment, particularly if it serves to free us from the corporate oligarchy."

"They suicided the MIT-Harvard scientist who announced that fusion was possible. He was a leftie and the gun was in his right hand," Larry interjected before changing the topic. "As for the islanders, that's why kava became their manna from heaven or holy communion rite. It brought them together in a peaceful way, though some became codependent and never seemed to move forward."

"I think Adam needed more than kava," Joan commented.

"Apparently he nourished insecurities," Larry remarked. "The Serpentines, Grays, and Blues all played on this."

Donna reiterated Larry's point, "The meaning of a symbol varies according to its context and content. Mental flexibility is key here rather than accepting disinformation and carving it into stone. It is even worse when they worship the stone. It is the key to deciphering the messages in the Horsetail Communication Network."

With these words, the discussion came to a gentle consensus. Everyone helped clean up after dinner. Then they exchanged affectionate good-byes and Larry and Joan went back to her cottage.

Later in the week, Carrie came to visit. She met Joan at the same seaside restaurant where Joan had broken up with Ernst.

"I sense things are coming full circle," she told Carrie as they relaxed after dinner and gazed out the window at the Atlantic ocean.

"Nobody knows when the time wrinkle will come full circle, though I think that somehow it became gridded with the Aztec calendar. The indigenous people are moving the energy forward. Many of the star seed people want nothing to do with the Serpentine Federation."

Joan felt the baby stir within her. She took a deep breath to collect herself before the nausea became overwhelming. Carrie studied her for a moment.

"I've decided to move in with Larry," Joan explained. "I've accepted a position with a slower-paced clinic that serves the area."

Carrie maintained her poker face while waiting for Joan to regain her composure.

"The Aztec calendar ends in 2012," Joan reminded her.

"I know," Carrie replied softly. " It is not the only calendar they made. They have others with different dates."

Joan watched Carrie's nonchalant shrug and pondered her reason.

"Truth is not kind," Carrie answered.

A small tear rolled down Joan's cheek. Carrie gently touched Joan's hands as if to ask for permission to hold them. Another tear escaped Joan's eye as she nodded at Carrie.

Carrie respectfully held Joan's hands in hers and gazed directly in Joan's eyes. "The time wrinkle differs from the Aztec calendar in that it is based on a Vision, one that involves free choice and free will. It is a bargain that has been part of this planet since the beginning of life as we know it." Then Carrie turned her attention to the view out the window. "It is like looking at a clear day and realizing that you've found clarity." Joan followed Carrie's stare out the window and then returned her attention to her hands, which Carrie still held. She brightly smiled at the warmth being expressed in front of her. Carrie returned her focus to the table and lightly stroked Joan's hands. Joan's tears ceased with the calming gesture. "FOREVER is the dream that was built into the time wrinkle," Carrie told her. She wanted to be sure that Joan understood her. "Like Vedic balance, it is a psychic defense. If you can see it, then you can dream it, and if you dream it, then you can create it. We are so much more than what we know or have known." Carrie released Joan's hands and sat back in her chair. She glanced at the vastness of the Atlantic Ocean before continuing, "We are more than our bodies, more than our brains or genitalia. More than our pain or suffering. There are more variables to add to the grand equation."

Joan noticed the flicker of pain that crossed Carrie's countenance as she spoke. Finally Joan understood. Carrie brushed her hand across her forehead as if to wave Joan away. "For these reasons, we must not get lost in our own reflections," Carrie went on.

Leaning closer to Carrie, Joan persisted, "My favorite psychology professor said that you only need one other person to have a shared reality. If one other person had the same experience, then you had a reality rather than an insanity."

"It is like taking a dive buddy along when you fathom the depths of consciousness," Carrie agreed.

Joan remained leaning over the table and kept Carrie in her focus. "What caused Brent's insanity?"

"He made a free choice to exclude anyone from his world. In the end, he could not get over himself. He didn't want to heal his own wound, much less acknowledge that he had one and was human."

Joan released Carrie in her mental hold and sat back in her chair. Clarity shone in her face and she had a determined air. She took another breath and addressed Carrie again. "Thank you for doing this."

In the infinity of time, Carrie understood Joan. "You know, that's the nicest thing anyone has ever told me. You are welcome," Carrie responded succinctly.

ADDENDUM
CHAPTER ONE

Impossible dreams

Are always short-lived

Due to their demand for action

Tune Reference: *The Impossible Dream*

----Jim Nabors

"OUR SON IS obsessed with dragons," Joan told Larry. "The only books he reads have pictures of dragons on the cover."

Larry glanced at her from the newspaper that he had been reading. He put down the paper and held one arm out for her as she sat down next to him on the couch. Smiling as he gently hugged her, Larry said, "You've noticed."

Joan smirked and looked into thin air. "Oden traded for several of Michael's clay dragons today at school. They were playing Town to learn commerce, and everyone had to make something to barter. Donna said that Michael's clay dragons are a sell out."

Larry stared at Joan and gave her a more persistent hug, "Sounds like Oden is not the only one who is fond of dragons." Then he deviated from the subject matter slightly, "Did you practice your Five Dragon exercise this afternoon?"

Joan focused on Larry, "I did. Another six days and I will be done with the hundred day period. Do you think the children are doing the training with me through osmosis?"

"It looks like it," Larry observed as he gazed at the sea outside the picture window. He could hear the rhythmic roll of waves as the tide came in. "We don't know how this *chi gung* practice works outside of the monasteries. One of my former classmates lost his mind with the Five Dragon set."

"So far, so good," Joan replied, joining Larry's gaze at the sea view. "The only thing I lost was a little bit of sleep trying to carve out time for doing the set, though the meditation helps me get by on less sleep. It is everyday for a hundred days. When it is over I am going to nap after the meditation exercise."

"Your easy success must be due to all the time we've spent tracking portals and communicating with merpeople,"Larry remarked.

Joan chuckled, "Well, we all have to start somewhere."

Then she closed her eyes and placed her head on Larry's shoulder. "My favorite set is the one where you end the meditation with a wide overhead arm sweep. What did YOU call it?...Baby dragon pops out of egg?"

Larry laughed at himself. Their casual, reflective moment was interrupted by a knock on the front door. Larry and Joan remained seated, while their son Oden answered the door. They recognized Donna's voice and Joan rose to greet her.

"Look, Mom!" Oden shouted. "Donna has a REAL dragon's egg!"

"Larry, please take a look at this," Donna pleaded. "I would have called ahead, but our phone is tapped again."

Larry got up from his comfortable seat on the sofa and hurried over to Donna. He lifted the egg-shaped crystal from her hands and placed it on the nearby dining table. Meanwhile, Michael, who had been following behind his mother, took Oden aside in a confidential manner. The boys retreated to Oden's bedroom with their whispered speculations about the origin and significance of the dragon's egg. Joan watched the boys disappear as Larry excitedly retrieved a magnifying glass from a drawer in the kitchen.

Joan shrugged at Donna, "We keep the magnifying glasses next to the forks in this house."

Donna laughed softly as she followed Larry. "It beats stethoscopes and law journals."

"You're right," Joan said, following Donna to the dining table.

"It is a fossilized creature," Larry decided. Continuing to peer through the magnifying glass, he questioned Donna, "Where did you get it?"

"Eli bought it from a poor merchant at a bazaar when he hiked around the Himalayans," Donna answered. "After undergraduate school, he traveled to Tibet. We were cleaning out his old spare office and I found this. Have you noticed that the kids have been playing with imaginary dragons lately?"

"So has Joan," Larry quipped.

"Oh, she must be doing the Five Dragon set," Donna commented, glancing at Joan. "No wonder, I felt compelled to bring this fossil over right away. She gets to transmute the energy."

Joan remained quiet. She left the room to collect her thoughts and check on her daughter and Carrie's son, who were playing together in the recreational room downstairs. Opening the door a little wider, she noticed that the two younger children had incorporated several dragons in their city of wooden blocks.

"Elissa is the Queen Dragon," Leandra told her playmate Vinnie. "That is why she is golden."

Joan stepped away from the doorway so that she would not be seen. She did not want to interrupt their happy child's play. She watched Leandra place the clay dragon on a ledge beside Vinnie's copper colored dragon with a Viking hat.

"Brunswick is ready to go on an ocean voyage with the Vikings. Earl can help Elissa watch the dragon cocoons," Vinnie rejoined.

"We need caretakers and flyers," Leandra added as she searched around her for human figurines.

Joan left the children and went back upstairs. She joined Larry and Donna standing around the dragon's egg at the dining table. They turned and looked at her.

"They are naming all the dragons now," Joan merely told them. "What do you call this bright green one?"

"Maybe we should ask the kids," Donna suggested.

Another thought crossed Joan's mind. Changing the subject, she asked, "Why is someone tapping your phone?"

Larry decided to brew some herb tea while Donna answered. Leaving the dragon egg on the dining table, he went into the kitchen where he could easily overhear the conversation. Donna nervously looked at Joan before responding.

"It has to do with the French alliance," Donna replied. "Apparently they wanted to assassinate both JFK and De Gaulle during the summer of 1961. Being half-French, Jacqueline accompanied him to France and ran intelligence operations. France would have been blamed for the assassinations. Her mother dated intelligence operatives and later married one.”

“Who are ‘they’?” Joan asked.

“The same group tapping our phone,” Donna answered. “Both Presidents wanted government-backed currency for their nations. JFK and De Gaulle served in underground intelligence operations during World War II.”

Larry handed the women their cup of tea as they sat down around the dragon egg to discuss this recent digression. Joan sensed that their conversation had something to do with the appearance of the dragon egg in their lives. She studied its intricate crystal pattern as she reflected on Donna’s words.

****

Five years later, Donna and Joan resumed the same conversation around the dragon egg.

“The younger generation is dubbing 9/11 as their Kennedy assassination,” Joan commented. She leaned back in her chair and sipped some green tea. “At the very least, it is more dead Irish.”

“It wasn’t as bad as we had anticipated,” Donna remarked. “Though they are criticizing the French for not joining the war. Eli says gold is missing from the Federal Reserve vaults. When Auchincloss reported missing gold from the Federal Reserve, she was found dead ten stories below her apartment. When JFK Jr. mentioned the empty vault at Fort Knox in his *George* magazine, he and his family died in a place crash a year and a half later.”

"It is more than just money," Joan observed as she studied the crystalized egg again. She had been repeatedly drawn to the mystery of the egg throughout the past five years. No one in the scientific community of Woodsport had been able to come up with an explanation of why the egg never hatched. "I feel like we are frozen in time like this egg."

Larry remained silent and nodded his agreement.

"I know." Eli sighed as he joined the group this time. "I think that the answer goes back to what Jackie said in response to a magazine interview shortly after the assassination."

"What do you mean?" Donna questioned.

"During the discussion, Jacqueline linked the assassination to Operation Camelot," Mark answered. "She wasn't just referring to the Camelot myth, which has a prominent dragon archetype. Jacqueline conveyed her awareness of the military's role in the assassination. Operation Camelot described a counter-presidency mission harbored at a nearby university run by Catholics. Many of the operatives were identified in Dealey Plaza on that day. These military men comprised the hawks of the Viet Nam war. They employed the shadowy underground that threatened the administrative branch of government since the early 1900's."

"Without justice, there are no laws," Joan added before pausing in reflection. "There are two premature babies buried with the Kennedys in Arlington National Cemetery," Joan recalled. "They are like this frozen egg. I think that there is a link here that we need to know. I think that is why it came into our lives while I trained with the Five Dragon set."

Larry spoke for the first time, "I think that it has something to do with the fact that this is not a Reptilian dragon. Don, our resident paleontologist, classified them as bird-like mammals. This dragon's wings are angelic."

"The past is the key to the future," Donna reminded them. "Everything remains trapped in a Hegelian dialectic. The legislative and judicial branch are inoperable. An obscure Midwest newspaper reported the Government Accounting Office found the 2004 election erroneous. Meanwhile, the courts play deaf. There is no way to correct a miscount without a majority in the legislature. The Federal Government is at loss to enforce the rules created by the people. Even Patrick Fitzgerald's investigation is frozen in time. Valerie Plame worked for a front company named after Auchincloss's benefactor. Brewster-Jennings is the name of a relative, who had worked with Standard Oil."

"Enough said," Larry quipped.

"Have they quit tapping your phone?" Joan asked, having grown accustomed to talking to Donna in code whenever she called.

"It comes and goes now, depending on what is happening in the news. When they have more stuff to hide, they tap more consistently.There is a familiar low vibrational frequency that we can detect when someone unwanted is listening. I have become sensitized and so has Eli."

"It is the connection to the earth spirit that they are after," Joan remarked, changing the subject slightly. "That is what dragons, Druids, and Free French have in common."

"That's it," Larry agreed. "The appearance of the dragon egg is a direct reference to the time wrinkle, which is aligned with the spirit of the earth."

Donna brightened before adding, "We are suspended in Time until events like 9/11 wrinkle their way out of the system coordinates."

Joan smiled, though she refused to take the situation lightly. "I think that it is too late for this little dragon to unfold. We still have a chance."

"It is an impossible mission," Larry commented. "This dragon egg tells us that we are over the edge."

"Well, it certainly has made our priorities different," Joan acknowledged.

****

Years later, after the first African-American president was inaugurated into office, Joan and her friends resumed their discussion around the dragon's egg. This time Carrie joined them. The year was 2009.

"We got through this event safely," Joan observed. "They say that the snow storm calmed everyone down. Washington D.C. experienced a week of relatively low crime as a result."

"Many Light Workers sent positive energy," Donna remarked. "Spiritual integrity bypasses HARRP anytime."

"HARRP?" Carrie questioned. "You don't think they actually have it working, do you?"

"Some think HARRP created Hurricane Katrina, Gustav, and Ike," Larry responded. "There's more to it. Evidence exists that someone dynamited the New Orleans dam."

"Like the drilling to the MidEarth, the potential for danger exists," Eli explained. "HARRP taps into the ionosphere."

"The ionosphere is where the Schumann Wave Guide is located," Donna remarked.

"The human brain can tap into the Schumann Waveguide through alpha waves," Joan continued.

"No more alpha surfing for my brain," Carrie joked.

"Just keep your spiritual integrity and you won't waver," Joan advised. "This is very ancient stuff. Remember, the Santas developed this waveguide as part of their communications network. Their free-floating civilization collapsed when the Serpentines found a way to manipulate it."

"Fortunately, man and woman do not live on alpha alone," Carrie quipped.

"There are three other frequencies known to be associated with the human brain," Joan explained. "Besides beta, delta, and theta frequencies the human brain might evolve a few new ones as a result."

"We could just filter and ground," Larry suggested. "It is simple radio theory."

Carrie laughed. "It really isn't conspiracy theory. It is Theoretical Physics. Some people major in it."

"Speaking of which," Joan interrupted. "Now that we are gathered around the dragon's egg again, tell us about how the time wrinkle is doing."

"The last burp or wrinkle was the tsunami of 2004," Carrie recalled. "A day after the earthquake, a huge burst of radiation came to Earth from a magnetar. A magnetar is a neutron star. It was the largest flux of incoming gamma rays ever known. We've been beamed by a magnetar over fifty thousand light years away."

"The tsunami had nothing to do with HARRP. It is about going to a higher frequency," Joan commented.

"At least we have some outside help," Eli acknowledged with a shrug at the dragon egg.

Joan stared thoughtfully at the dragon egg. After pausing briefly, she summarized, "We are incorporating a utopic vision of the world. Little did we know that we were reaching for that unreachable star."

ADDENDUM
CHAPTER TWO

Kindness is what

It is all about

Whereas the pursuit of pleasantries

With all token accoutrements of social status

Take us further

From a meaningful life

Tune Reference: *Pleasant Valley Sunday*

----The Monkees

"SEVERAL OF MY patients came in with the most odd cough," Joan began as she sipped her green tea.

"What is so unusual about the cough?" Donna questioned, gazing outside the cafe window at the surf.

"It appears the pathogen infiltrated the host to the core," she explained. "It was like a direct hit on the DNA."

"Is that what they mean by cold wind penetrates *Chi* in Chinese Medicine?" Donna asked.

"The patients only seem to respond to homeopathics and botanicals, the substances that protect the DNA. I have a homeopath on staff now."

"The treatments with the best historical track record on epidemics consist of Chinese herbs and homeopathy," Donna commented. She leaned forward with a slight tease, "Bloodletting won't do this time. I used Oscillococcinum for the swine flu. The New England Journal of Medicine reported its effectiveness years before the epidemic."

"Yes, I know. I used it too," Joan confessed. "This latest winter cough is much different. What do you know about nanotechnolgy?"

"Some researchers have speculated about the use of nanotechnology in genocide. They can use it to target genetic lines. I think that it is still in the theoretical stages," Donna answered before she gulped her chamomile tea.

Both women paused to gaze at the sea. Several seagulls soared in the air above the cafe on the pier. Some were diving in the surf and returning with tidbits of seafood.

Donna looked down at the table and moved her napkin in a circular pattern. "My friend Eric told me about SANTS yesterday. It is a nanotechnology project funded by the European Union."

"Sants, hmm," Joan reflected. "That is the last name of one of Nicholas's cousins. They were related to King Ceredig, who claimed parenthood of Saint David of Wales. Although they considered St. David as a relation, I gathered that his mother had been violated, which casts doubt on Ceredig's claims. The local natives called David, Dewi."

"It was a popular trend for the remaining Roman soldiers to align themselves with the religious authority of Constantinople. Many assumed names like Xavier, Sanctus, and Christian," Donna continued. "Meanwhile, the native Druids fled to the monasteries where they were later canonized, which is the equivalent of a spiritual violation."

"After what I saw this week in the clinic, I'm not ready to nominate SANTS for sainthood, much less research funding," Joan agreed. "It is like putting the word *holy* in front of 'roman empire.' "

"Eli says that SANTS is no more than the holy roman empire in its ancient Serpentine form." Donna nodded at Joan. "Both use invasive techniques to spread itself. SANTS wants to infiltrate diatoms with nanotechnology."

"It is a carcinogen in the making. Carrie told me that their physics lab had found it in the matrix of the soda water that they tested," Joan admitted. "My herbalist gave me the Diatom sea essence last week. She told me that it was to restore light energy to the cells."

"Call it cellular dharma, an enlightened cell." Donna smiled. "I have another bit of synchronicity for you. Eric obtained a few diatoms last week and found that he could activate them in such a way that they had anti-cancer properties. The cells had greater immunity."

"Immunity from what?" Joan asked in a loud whisper. She leaned closer to Donna to let her know that she wanted the full story.

Donna pulled away and nervously waved her hands in small circles in front of Joan. She took a deep sigh and explained, "Somebody sent Carrie a gift wrapped with ribbon containing nanotechnology. She finally figured out why she had such low immunity all these years, though the contamination fades with time." Donna dropped her hands to the table and took a relaxed breath. "Eric experimented with the contaminated ribbon and the diatoms. You know, I can see why diatoms are called Light Spirits. They are immortal. It was their phosphorescent shimmer that guided one of the space shuttles back to earth."

"There is no place like home," Joan murmured.

"Don't remind me," Donna interjected. "Our mission concerning the dragon egg is about bringing heaven to earth. The diatoms are our allies. We have help."

"Here goes to a few solutions," Joan proposed as she raised her green tea in a sincere toast.

Donna quietly nodded her agreement without moving her teacup. She didn't want to call attention to their table. Joan noticed her wariness and motioned questionably towards the door. Donna briefly extended five fingers on the table, encouraging Joan to wait a few more minutes more. Then they left the cafe after some light conversation.

Donna and Joan walked over to the far end of the pier where they could not be overheard. The wind and the surf easily drowned out their words. Joan noticed a light shimmering over the ocean before them and saw the merpeople in the far distance.

"I am going to a cousin's wedding in Arizona," Donna said. It will be held at the church where her parents' married. It is called Mission San Xavier. The Jesuits named it for one of their founders. When the King of Spain began to distrust the Jesuits, he banned them from the Americas and gave the mission to the Franciscans. This occurred less than 10 years before the American Revolution in 1776. The Franciscans were considered more reliable and the church became later known as the white dove of the desert. Fifty years later, Mexico banned the Spanish and the local Indians took care of it until the U.S. bought the land in time for the Civil War."

Joan stared at Donna with wide eyes. "What are you going to do for protection? You are coming out of hiding."

"Probably the same thing that Carrie did when she presented her physics paper at the Russian Academy of Biophysics. I'll take a few protective devices like the Clarus from Stanford Research and an inert gas device from Pegasus Products. Fred at Pegasus Products said that the researchers almost decided to combine the two into one medal."

Donna leaned casually on the rail and began humming *Back in the USSR*, a popular Beatles song.

"Is Eli going?" Joan asked.

"No, they would mess with him for sure. We both picked up that vibe and another obligation came up. Luckily, the kids are in college and can't take the time off. As much as we all would love to go and see everyone, it has the words "set up" printed in invisible ink on the invitations."

"What about Carrie?" Joan quizzed Donna. "When is it? I think I have a conference in Arizona during early November."

"The wedding is the first weekend in November," Donna said as she seriously considered meeting Joan during the trip.

"Sounds like a gridding opportunity to me," Joan concluded. "We'll have fun."

Donna smiled, appearing slightly relieved. "Fun is the best protective device around. We'll see a few geologic formations, maybe some cacti, great Mexican food, and a margarita..."

"It's a deal," replied Joan, staring out at sea again as she changed the subject. "Let's go visit the art fair up the street."

Donna nodded and they walked off the pier for the concrete sidewalks of the coastal town. They passed by shops and smiling pedestrians on the sunny spring day. The wind had died down and conversations could be easily heard.

"This would be a nice night for some astronomy," Donna remarked. "We could call up Carrie and see if she has her eight inch telescope out tonight. She told me that there was an alignment consisting of Regulus, the Moon, and Mars in the southern sky tonight. It will be a beautiful clear night."

"Let's see what stars we can find at the art fair, first. Yanni gave me an Earth Keeper crystal last week," Joan mentioned. "I am carrying it in my pocket."

"What is an Earth Keeper crystal?" Donna asked as they walked uphill to the street with the art fair.

"It is a crystal that contains information about the earth since its beginning. Some say they were around after Atlantis sank, but I think they have been around longer. They also serve as portals and connect with the energetic network of the planet. They are great for gridding and for communication. Some of the crystals attract each other like male-female connectors on an electronics circuit."

"Given these auspices, it should be interesting to see what we connect with at the art fair," Donna remarked.

The women walked the aisles of the art fair. A man hawking a free raffle persuaded Joan to enter the drawing, while Donna's attention was drawn to some acrylic discs at an adjacent table. She talked briefly to the artist about his original geometric creations called Light Energy Discs. Then she caught up with Joan and they crossed the aisle to other exhibits.

"You really should go see the artist with the energy templates," Donna suggested after they had toured most of the exhibits on the other side.

Her words were interrupted by the man with the raffle. "Joan Standish, you win a Light Energy Disc."

Joan looked up at the hawker as he repeated her name. Donna encouraged her to move towards him and collect the two inch disc that could be worn as a necklace. Joan obtained the disc and stood for a moment admiring the design.

"Let's go see the artist," Joan whispered to Donna. "It's a portal concerning the star Regulus. The artist is a messenger."

Donna led Joan back to the artist that she had met earlier. A young blonde haired man rose from his chair and smiled in greeting. Still far enough to avoid being overheard, Donna quietly said to Joan, "The artist is a time traveler from Regulus."

"Is he one of the Three Wise Men?" Joan asked with a perplexed look on her face.

"There were at least thirty Kings connected to that star sphere that encircled the globe under the energetic traction of Regulus," Donna explained. "Carrie and Jasper came over one Christmas with their telescope. There was a portal and we got the story."

"Oh," Joan said almost absentmindedly as she approached the time traveler. Carrie had married Jasper many years ago and together they had two children slightly younger than Joan and Larry's. Before she neared the table, Joan said softly in Donna's ear, "He does seem celestial."

"At least more than human," Donna quietly replied.

Joan presented her win to the artist.

"You won the Angelic Shield Disc," he told her after he studied the disc.

"I need the Angelic Shield Disc," she admitted with a laugh.

"Great, I'll take the big six-inch disc over there," Donna interjected.

"That one is the Archangelic Shield Disc," he replied. "If you need amplification I have these two other discs over here. Each has a different design center."

"Now I know what I will be taking to the wedding in Arizona," Donna observed. "I want to buy a White Light Shield Disc for Eli. I'll send the kids in college some of the two inch ornaments."

"What do you have for gridding an Earth Keeper crystal with formations in Arizona?" Joan asked in her characteristic casual, direct manner.

Without a blink, the artist pointed to a purple disc off to the side. "This is the one I've been working on lately. It is for evolution of consciousness. We can incorporate some of the other designs in the template."

Joan examined the purple disc in front of her. She noticed that the design contained the Diamond Conscious Disc. She could feel herself lapsing into the energy of the portal.

"How about adding this amplifier template for greater coherency along with the Harmonic Resonator Disc?" she asked.

The artist place the acrylic discs on top of each other and examined the resulting design. Both Joan and Donna observed the effect. They turned and nodded at each other in agreement.

"I'll finish it up and send it to you," the artist offered.

Joan beamed with delight and they closed the deal. He carefully wrapped their purchases in blankets of soft white felt and the women went on their way. They strolled out of the art fair and headed back to their car parked a few streets away.

When they were alone inside the car, Joan suggested, "Let's determine what effect these templates have on objects contaminated with nanotechnology."

Donna nodded her agreement. "Eric may be in his lab today. We can also determine whether they protect organisms from nanotechnology effects. Already, Eric has discovered that certain crystals such as black tourmaline offer protection from the negative energy. You must have a big enough crystal though."

"That is what I like when I feel surrounded by problems. Solutions," Joan admitted after she pulled out of the parking space. She sped down the road past the art fair. "It is always nice to have a little synchronicity, too. Not to mention luck."

A few days later, Joan received a call from Donna. "The Angelic Shield Disc offers protection from the nanotechnology effects. Eric investigated the template with the contaminated ribbon and diatoms. We have solutions."

ADDENDUM

CHAPTER THREE

Being in the wrong place

At the right time

Can light up the darkness

Of the other path

Missed by sophomoric fools

Tune Reference: *Fool In The Rain*

----Led Zeppelin

A BLAST OF warm air greeted Joan as she walked outside the Arizona airport to the autumn conference scheduled at a resort a few minutes away. Planning to meet Donna, who happened to be at the family wedding nearby, she noticed that her friend had left a text message on her cell phone. After waiting to respond until she had obtained the rental car, Joan attempted to understand Donna's message. She made a quick phone call to Donna before leaving the car lot. In so many words, Donna had discretely texted for assistance.

"Hi Donna, I'm here in Arizona. How about taking a hike tomorrow after breakfast?" Joan asked. "What's on your mind?"

"I don't fell safe here and there is no place to go.for help. Let's do some gridding. How about going to the Canelo Hills?" "Some think that there is a volcanic caldera there. It is near the headwaters of the Santa Cruz River."

"I'll call your room after I enter the hotel. It will be about ten in the morning. Stay there until I find you. Collect your things. You can stay with me."

The next morning, Joan took the elevator to Donna's floor after calling first. She knocked on the door to Donna's room. Immediately, Donna opened the locked door wide for her. Without a word, Donna quickly ushered Joan inside the room and gestured to the giant dark wooden medallion hanging from a wall in the room. Then she pointed to the trap doors in the ceiling. Every room of the suite had one. One of the windows was directly across an office building. Any one with a pair of binoculars would be able to see directly inside the room. Donna closed the drapes on the windows and left the lights on in the room. Then the women quietly exited the hotel. Donna trailed a few steps behind Joan so that it was not obvious that they were together. When they arrived at the parked rental car along the street, Joan hurriedly unlocked the doors and they hopped in. They drove out of the city of Tucson towards the mountains.

"Your hotel room reminds me of the *Zorro* movies," Joan said. "Isn't that medallion on the wall a symbol associated with the religious occult?"

"Like Zorro, they left their mark in every room. Some little factory in Mexico made a killing with the design," Donna remarked. "And now they want to kill us. Eli cautioned me about not taking my laptop on this trip."

"I agree with Eli's intuition," Joan responded. "Good thing Carrie is staying with her aunt in town. Where did they have the wedding reception?"

"They had a catered dinner and dance in the lobby of a bank. I'm sure that they had all the bank cameras on. Talk about a show stopper. Most relations pretended that we really were not that well-connected. It was so obvious to everyone in the family. Carrie and I only talked to each other at the church," Donna commented, before elaborating further. "All the place settings had boxes of chocolate tied with shiny ribbons. The ribbons looked exactly like the one I gave Eric for his experiments with nanotechnology. It aroused my suspicions and I never untied the ribbon on my box. They ribbons were tracking devices. It identifies the work of the *nadas* involved in crashing the bank system."

"Looks like the conquistadors have returned," "We all should be carrying black tourmaline where we keep our money--purses, wallets, *feng shui* areas for prosperity.

"The bank building is owned by a company that owns the server for the bank."

Joan took a deep breath before she began, "OK, aside from the personal peril, there are some major portents here."

"Yes, financial terrorism. In the past month, Eli and I have changed banks, servers, and email addresses. After the wedding, we are going to change retirement funds, financial advisors, and accountants."

"We all need to change. You are lucky that you get a preview of what is to come," Joan commented as she turned off the highway and drove to the trail at the base of the mountains. "Let's go gridding."

"We are adding the enlightenment of the original savior movement to the network," Donna surmised as she surveyed the terrain. "It is the energy of Regulus, the star associated with the Wise Men."

Joan chuckled. "Obviously, they are seeking balance in having two women do the gridding in the present."

Donna shrugged at Joan. "Let's just go with it." Donna forged ahead on the uphill trail and added, "It is the Roman lions who are almost extinct now, not the Christians. Rome fell and the coliseum remains in ruins."

Joan, following Donna up the mountain. When they reached the top, they sat down on rocky ledge and enjoyed lunch. With delight, Donna pulled out two yogurt containers from a backpack and placed them on a handkerchief. The attendant from the buffet had given them to her for her hike.

"How did Carrie's relations get mixed up with the far-right-religious-crusading-military-industrial-complex?" Joan asked.

Donna smirked at Joan's worded description, and ignored the question. "Let's take out the Earth Keeper crystal and track the information. I have a crystal from the Himalayas that I think will fit it. We can put the connected crystals over two of the Light Energy Discs."

Joan placed Donna's Himalayan crystal in a slot on the Earth Keeper crystal and found that it fit perfectly. She placed the crystal arrangement on the acrylic templates between them. Joan turned towards Donna and studied the mountain view in the distance behind her.

"Eli's investigations have suggested that only two of the signers of the Declaration of Independence were not corrupted by the English bankers," Donna explained. "The English bankers also managed funds for the Vatican. One of the signers of the Declaration of Independence had a cousin who gridded Washington D.C. according to the Vatican. Church and state were separated only on paper for the new location of the country's capitol. The capitol resembles St. Peter's basilica in many ways. Done by design rather than by accident, it represents a very different look from the quaint Independence Hall in Philadelphia, which still contains the portraits of the

King and Queen of France. These monarchs funded the American Revolution only to lose their heads in the French Revolution when the U.S. moved its capitol to Washington D.C.. The land had been owned and surveyed by a cousin of one of the signers."

"Sounds like a conflict of interest," Joan remarked.

"Maybe. The younger brother of the man who surveyed Washington D.C. served as a Jesuit. He became the first bishop in America. The pope had banned the Jesuits in 1773. Complete with a new basilica, Washington D.C. became a haven for Jesuit refugees."

Donna took a deep breath and then continued, "It is no coincidence that thousands of unknown French soldiers and sailors were buried near this family's estate in Maryland. Nobody knows what happened and the French soldiers remain unknown in history as well. I am sure that the French could have used these soldiers in protecting their own government a few years later."

"The political currents ran much deeper than the monarchies. It was about power and greed."

"This religious sect that gridded the capitol for this nation had relatives that intermarried with Carrie's relations," Donna continued. "Carrie told me that they were also Brent's ancestors. She recognized the names on the tombstones found in the same graveyard at church where her grandparents married."

"I'm ready to head down the mountain now," Joan interrupted as she collected her Earth Keeper crystal from the template. "I think our job is done here. Let's go rest at my place. You can always make random appearances at the hotel to make them think that you are still there."

Donna rose from her position with a slight shudder at the thought of returning to the hotel room. She looked at the terrain below them. Nodding before she took a few steps down the mountain, she told Joan, "I think I'll take you up on that offer, given the history."

ADDENDUM

CHAPTER FOUR

There's nothing like the

Scent of a breeze

To let you know that

You are on the correct path

Tune Reference: *Nothing Left To Lose*

Mat Kearney

"SO THEY WANT to kill me for all those guitar masses that I did as a teenager," Carrie summarized after listening to Donna's account of the wedding in Arizona. She casually paced the floor of Joan's living room, where they had regrouped after the trip. "Being young and foolish, I overlooked the relations who let the killers in."

"Based on clinical observation and biological theory, this type of nanotechnology exposure creates cancer," Joan told her. "How long have you been receiving these shiny ribbons as gifts?"

"Ever since I survived the time wrinkle," Carrie admitted. "Maybe that is why one of my great-uncles suddenly came down with a rare form of cancer a few months after the last family reunion, near the time that Brent shifted to a negative family pattern."

Joan threw up her hands and walked over to stare out the picture window in the dining room. The dragon's egg had been moved to the side. Joan didn't bother gazing at it this time. Instead, she left to prepare some herbal tea for her friends after indulging in a brief change of scenery. Donna decided to stand up too. She went to help Joan in the kitchen and retrieve cups for their tea. Carrie left her seat also.

After spending a few moments pacing in front of the picture window, Carrie proposed, "I'll go pick up something for lunch, while you both stay here. What would you like?"

After Carrie left, Donna resumed the discussion, "Eli's latest investigation has led him to some of Mae Brussel's research on musicians."

Joan blinked, sensing a link between the research and Carrie's guitar masses. She stared at the floor as Donna continued.

"Apparently, the 1975 Senator Frank Church Committee Hearings and FBI counter-intelligence programs successfully documented the intent to break up the new Left. After the phenomenon of Woodstock, they targeted music festivals. People who sing and talk about peace and love become spiritual forces in the world for positive change."

Joan thought about Donna's words and nodded silently. She sipped her tea and motioned Donna to sit down at the counter. Recalling how many wonderful people she knew that had mysteriously died under illogical circumstances, she sighed and sat down near Donna. Then she acquiesced, "Those who tamper with ribbons and put GMOs in food, certainly would not stop at poisoning drinks, contaminating drugs, tampering with planes, and other people's minds."

"Mae Brussel's list includes Jim Croce, Jimi Hendrix, Mama Cass, Janis Joplin, Tim Buckley, Jim Morrison, and at least twenty others," Donna pointed out. "The sudden deaths during the peak of an artist's career are usually followed by character assassinations. Mae Brussel's own daughter died in a mysterious car accident. Shortly afterwards, Mae died quickly from cancer."

"Health officials want to resume putting fluoride in the water," Joan interjected, after thinking about the musicians. "Most people don't realize that the Nazis fluoridated the water in the ghettos to control the masses so that they could be herded like sheep to the death camps. There's documentation."

"Luckily, Carrie has some people running interference for her."

"Luckily, she likes to eat vegetables." Joan added as Carrie returned with the take out. "I was just getting around to discussing all the anticancer properties of vegetables."

"Keep telling me how healthy I am," Carrie responded dryly.

"The next two generations are very mystifying," Joan remarked, slightly changing the subject once she started enjoying her meal. "They call them the Indigo Kids and the Crystal Children."

"A psychologist called the next generation Indigo Kids because their aura had a distinct indigo color present," Donna added. "The term remains controversial in scientific research. I find the term useful in describing how a particular age group responds to its environment."

"The phenomenon is not new," Carrie agreed. "Some kids are duds like their parents, while others choose aliveness. The Indigo Kid has a harder world to navigate than we did. Technology has advanced so rapidly that they need to be able to keep up in way that is grounded and connected. It is amazing to watch the younger generation personalize it. They can take something that is cold, hard, and steely and use it for warm fuzzy energy.

They have turned a big complicated world into a smaller one with Facebook, Tweeter, email, and iPhones."

Joan smiled, "They work quickly, too. They are like little magicians. In contrast to Generation X or the Matrix Culture, they sense the energy of the planet on a very intuitive level. Most are passionately environmental."

"What about the Crystal Children?" Donna asked, staring out the window.

"These younger children are already enlightened," Carrie remarked. "They were born after 9/11 and had to process that trauma to get beyond the dissociation. Some of the Indigos mature into Crystal Children by the time they reach college. Others get stuck in confusion and repeat old negative, inherited patterns. Drugs don't work for them; they require nature-based modalities."

Joan linked the topic to their preceding discussion, "Every child of today must navigate authorities and institutions that have a history of character assassination and annihilation of spirit. We are not just talking about depersonalized, dehumanizing experiences. The stakes are bigger."

"They are born in a society that promotes the antihero. Christ-like qualities must be buried deep in the personalities at a survival level," Carrie observed. "This antichrist has been around for a very long time. It is anti-earth spirit."

"The Crystal Children work with a planet that has already gone over the edge," Donna surmised. "These are the ones who rise to the challenge of the time wrinkle. They look inside for answers, because they realize that they are not going to find them anywhere else. They follow their own star, having already realized their own mission or agenda at birth."

Carrie raised her cup of tea, "I propose a toast to those parents who figure their kids out. It is a tough job, but somebody's gotta be creative."

"Here, here," Joan and Donna echoed as they joined cups with Carrie's. "To college Moms!"

No sooner had their cups dropped, then Larry excitedly entered the kitchen. He carried a heavily wrapped bundle and carefully sat it down on the counter. He quickly kissed Joan and began ripping the paper from the package.

"How was your geologic expedition in the French Alps?" Joan asked.

"All remained calm here," Donna commented. "No sign of Nicholas and his assets."

Without a word, Larry delightedly exposed the pink dragon's egg underneath the wrapping.

"There are two now," Donna said. "I wonder what this pink one represents."

"We were talking about parenting the next generation" Joan reminded her. "This pink egg is a reminder to stay on track. It is time to teach our adult children how to grid properly and use portal etiquette."

"Then there is the code," Donna added, cocking her head quietly side to side as if weighing the possibility.

"What code?" Joan asked.

"The one that I use when I am modeling seismic data or evaluating a situation in real life," she said.

"What do you mean?" Joan questioned her.

"Well, it communicates information to the twenty-second dimension," Donna explained. "I just sorta picked it up. Zero and One are symbols for the feminine and masculine. Two refers to partnership. For example, we have two eggs. The message is that we are in partnership with the energy of the dragons."

Everyone in the room quieted and nodded for her to continue.

"Four is a writing number," Donna quietly resumed. "Five is a regal number. Six is an earthy number, good or bad depending on the context. Seven is a sacred number. Eight represents time. Nine pertains to the inverse."

"No pun intended, but it is all beginning to add up," Carrie remarked in a serious voice.

ADDENDUM

CHAPTER FIVE

The fountain of youth

Is found by

Those willing to

Reject the wrongful choices

Of a blind status quo

Tune Reference: *Bennie And The Jets*

----Elton John

"IT IS A French dragon," Joan commented as she studied the fossilized egg along with the others.

"There is something to know about France," Carrie interjected. "It is a message for us in the present."

"We still don't know what stopped the incubation," Larry reminded them.

"I think that it has something to do with *The Prince*," Donna said out loud. "I have been referred to that book three times in the past week."

"Are you referring to Machiavelli's book?" Larry asked. "He wrote it after being tortured and banned from political office by the Medici. Some dismiss it as comical satire, while others study it seriously. Stalin slept with a copy of it by his bed."

"No, I mean the children's version," Donna replied. "The one about a child getting bit by a snake while he recovered from a heartache. In the end he is dehumanized, and goes back to live in isolation on an asteroid with a thorny rose. The aviator in the story doesn't have a clue about the type of care that a child needs. He treats the child like an alien from outer space."

"Sounds very Serpentine to me," Joan commented.

"It is," Donna retorted. "Saint wrote the book in NY before joining De Gaulle's forces and then disappeared. De Gaulle suspected Saint of supporting the Nazis. He had many German admirers, including a Luftwaffe pilot who claimed that he shot his plane down. The plane turned out to be American."

"It is Gray issue," Carrie observed. "Grays are associated with the depersonalized style of the Nazis."

"The kids never did like that story," Joan admitted.

"The French never did like the US government's story of 9/11," Donna stated.

"It cost them some public support," Joan pointed out. "We all must hold steady."

"There's another WWII link," Donna observed. "The attack targeted the assassinated president's former office in WWII. He had initially worked for the Office of Naval Intelligence before officially going to the Pacific. An officer from Naval Intelligence was jailed in Canada and predicted that the Pentagon would be hit. They were investigating the 1991 economic coup of the Soviet Union. Western companies gained control of the Soviet oil and mineral reserves through the rise of Yeltsin. Minsk, the town where the alleged assassin stayed in Russia, has very rich oil reserves."

"Ancestors of the US President during 9/11 had funded and traded with the Nazis during WWII. According to the Department of Justice, they profited from the labor at Auschwitz," Larry added. "Relations of the slain president at Standard Oil used profits to fund the American Eugenics Society. After Lenin came to power, Standard Oil gained access to Russian oil. The Minsk oil reserves were managed by alleged assassin's handler, a triple agent who had also dated the slain president's mother-in-law. The Nazis occupied Minsk during WWII."

Carrie continued, "Now I know why Stalin shot his cabinet. Some of the Russians that I met in Moscow called it progress, whereas the tour guide and his driver called it a crime. The building where they lived remains unoccupied to this day. There is a big Mercedes Benz symbol on top of it. I could not help but think that it was demoralizing to the populace."

"His real name was Jughashvili. He chose Stalin, which means steel, while he was organizing riots in the oil fields of Baku. The people who owned Standard Oil also sat on the board of directors for US Steel Corp, which also had offices in Russia. Remember that one of our US presidents helped build the Moscow-St. Petersburg train. John Quincy Adams's infant daughter is buried in St. Petersburg. Adams stayed there during Napoleon's invasion, which British bankers funded for the French. After ousting the Welsh Druids, the British bankers funded the Russians as well and they eventually owned Russia's oil by the turn of the century."

A knock on the door interrupted their discussion concerning the pink dragon's egg. Larry went to answer the knock. The rest remained lost in thought for a few moments.

"Hi Jasper, come on in!" Larry greeted. "Your wife is in the kitchen with the new dragon's egg that I brought from my survey in the French Alps."

Jasper, a muscular, dark-haired man entered the room. His love of astrophysics had led him to Carrie, who he adored even more. Curiously, he glanced sideways at Larry and entered the kitchen without further questions. He carried a flyer from a Boston museum in his hands.

"They didn't respect the significance of the artifact," Larry explained. "For the others in the survey, the rock has no value."

"The scientists must have been Serpentine," he insisted before greeting his wife with a tender kiss on the lips. "Their loss is our gain."

"What do we have here?" Carrie questioned as she reached for the art flyer in Jasper's gentle hands.

"It is for an art exhibit on Japanese textiles," he told her as he examined the group gathered around the pink dragon egg.

"Oh look, these Japanese robes for firefighters are amazing!" Carrie exclaimed. She leaned over the counter to study the pictures in the flyer.

"We were just talking about firefighters and first responders," Joan said, synchronistically tying the discussion.

"These robes are padded to protect the firefighter," Donna commented as she looked over Carrie's shoulder. "After balance has been restored to the burning site, the firefighter ceremoniously reverses the coat to reveal the beautiful embroidery on the inside. This coat has a dragon design on it. The dragon is spewing a jet of water in the air."

Everyone stared at the dragon's egg again and compared it to the embroidered design.

"We still don't know what stopped this egg from hatching," Larry interrupted after a moment of silence. "In the ancient Asian traditions, firefighters were considered the spiritual elite. As celebrated healers they restored Vedic balance to the elements. Elements such as water, earth, and wood were manipulated to bring harmony to an area with too much fire energy. The better firefighters sported coats like a knight with a decorated coat of arms or a high school letter jacket."

"The spiritual warriors of 9/11 balanced the heavy materialism associated with the tragedy. Humanity swarmed in to help with this dehumanizing, depersonalizing assault," Joan reflected. "The secondary assault occurred when the Christ-like compulsion was answered with a trap, much like the musicians of Mae Brussel's research. I don't think the firefighters expected the building to crumple with all their years of experience in steel and glass. It did not involve the element of wood in this modern city. This was a different ballgame."

Larry nodded at his wife before planting a kiss on her cheek. "I think we got it. We've transmuted the energy with the understanding. The message of the dragon's egg is to use our intuition and keep moving forward."

"Most scientists and engineers do not buy the government's account," Donna remarked. The buildings were probably detonated with the plastic explosives that were made by the company that Eli investigated. The production was done under hypnosis. Most amusement parks can make a plane look like it is crashing into a building. We took the kids there the month before 9/11. The evening laser light show appears very convincing. Skolnick, the real man behind the *Ironside* character, investigated the connection between Disney, Coca Cola, Supreme Court, and 9/11. Raymond Burr played the wheelchair-bound detective after his stint in *Perry Mason.*

"We need to let the kids know what is real and what is smoke and mirrors," Donna added. "As parents, we need to nurture this intuitive process as well as the time wrinkle."

"There's more to balance," Carrie interjected. "The tower of Babel becomes an archetype. The destruction of a phallic symbol alludes to the intergalactic wars of ancient Egypt."

Joan thought about her words and agreed, "You're right. The time wrinkle departs from the symbology used in ancient Egypt, whereas other places such as Washington D.C. and a few colleges have resurrected that connection with obelisks. Although considered a phallic symbol, they are said to represent petrified rays of the sun disk. There's another metaphorical connection to the petrified egg on this table."

"Don't look back at the destruction or else you'll become stone," Carrie summarized.

"That's the third assault," Joan remarked. "The degree of secondary trauma is so intense that it kills."

"It is a form of mental manipulation," Larry commented.

Joan collapsed in a chair near the counter. "That explains why Aconite has been so successful with the flu lately. It is a homeopathic given to the little old lady types who witness scenes like car wrecks. It has a big fear keynote and is also used for skiers who develop a cough when the dry Colorado air penetrates their lungs. In this area, it is for people who get a cough from sitting near dry air vents or air conditioning."

"During WWI, studies were done at the Tavistock Institute to determine how much a soldier could take before their mental health was unrecoverable," Donna added.

"Reminds me of a Batman movie," Larry remarked.

"Reminds me of the hazardous waste company that we investigated," Donna rejoined. "Larry thinks that there is a connection between those people who were hypnotized and 9/11. Through hypnosis, traumatized employees made bombs from illegal hazardous substances, later forgetting what they had done. Instead, other countries were blamed. Hindsight isn't always 20-20 vision in this case, especially if the memory is laced with trauma. People tend to remember the emotion."

"Reruns can be hypnotic," Joan observed. "In combination with hypnosis or dissociation, the trauma becomes programmed in the psyche. Sometimes it becomes a self-fulfilling prophesy."

"Or self-destructive," Larry speculated.

"It is like playing with fire," Carrie added. "Firefighters tell that to all the kids."

"Other things are difficult to avoid," Donna admitted. "We are all vulnerable. We must cultivate our awareness skills and avoid trouble, like defensive driving. Some people don't think that it was a coincidence that one of the buses in the London bombing exploded at the door of Tavistock. The street sign in the picture of a Chicago newspaper read 'Greys Inn' or Grays in."

"And heal our wounds from the past, which brings us to Planet Nibu," Carrie surmised. She explained, "It is the planet associated with Donna's code. It is in the twenty-second dimension. I made a portal for the connection when I visited the Big Four Ice Caves during a trip to Washington state. There is a vortex there that connects to Sol Duc Hot Springs in the Washington rain forest."

"So that is where you get all those extraterrestrials from the twenty-second dimension?" Joan speculated.

"Some things are just natural," Carrie answered. "Ancient civilizations called the Planet Nibiru, which is a technical term in Babylonian astronomy. It is known also as the Planet of the Crossing for December 2012."

"This timing corresponds to the Mayan calendar," Joan remarked.

"Whatever has been incubating in the twenty-second dimension gets birthed by the Winter Solstice of 2012," Carrie continued. "It is almost like a soul retrieval, except this is associated with the ancient gridding of Gondwanaland."

"We'll get to that later," Larry insisted. "I am busy understanding the language of numbers. We must be in the middle of an inverse or number 9 moving in a number 2 partnership with the dragon eggs towards a more sacred 7."

"Unlike the furry dragons, which birth their young like kangaroos, the sea dragons reproduce like turtles and birds. The furry dragons went to the MidEarth as the sea dragons evolved and brought heaven to earth. We are moving back to the garden and freedom, while we keep one foot in the present and another in the past. As we leave our state of suspension, we gain greater awareness." Joan smiled with a wink to everyone gathered around her. Without saying anything more, the group at the table silently dispersed. After a few friendly hugs, they left to sleep on the matter overnight.

ADDENDUM

CHAPTER SIX

Humanity died in the 1960's

Nature died in the 1970's

This world is winding down

The new one must be created

Out of love and joy

Rather than duress

This is the secret of the century

Marked by end of the Mayan calendar

Signaling the end of the wasteful human sacrifice

No more dust to dust

A new vision of ourselves

Lends itself to a new planet

Tune Reference: *A New World Coming*

----Mama Cass Elliot

SEVERAL DAYS LATER, Joan stood in front of the energetic template in her home. She carefully probed the depths of the portal for signs of any intrusions. Reaching the end, she found that she remained unharmed. The portal stopped abruptly at the Gray's base three hundred miles off the coast of Greenland. The location corresponded to the site on Larry's map.

For a brief moment Joan sensed the austere, cold, northern landscape in a bunk deep beneath a wandering ice flow. A plump fair-skinned woman greeted her. She had dark hair and wore a ruby red strapless dress. Remaining perched on her cushion against the steely gray wall of the corridor, the woman flashed a wicked smile at Joan. She waved a golf-ball sized ruby ring in the air and Joan immediately backed off.

"I have the red ruby ring," she mocked.

Joan studied the situation and unmasked her enemy. She quickly summoned Carrie's extraterrestrials to defuse the potentially explosive confrontation. In a quick flash of lightning the woman thrusted the ruby ring in Joan's hand before dissolving into the nothingness.

"You win," the dark-haired woman told her with a hideous laugh as if she didn't care whether came or went. "The ruby red ring is yours."

Joan examined the red ring suspiciously. It reminded her of a patient that she had seen the other day.This patient had been experiencing secondary trauma relating to the Japanese tsunami. Somehow this ring had become linked with the patient. Trusting this positive connection, Joan hung on to that memory as the ring faded into the twenty-second dimension, leaving a permanent energetic imprint in her possession.

She recalled the dream about the red ruby ring that she had had last night. The ring in her dream was part of another important gridding system, one that was foreign to her. She had regained the ring from the Grays who stole it from the Regulus civilization. Joan sensed the trauma that the Grays had inflicted on the original owners of the red ring. The grossly obese woman, who had handed her the red ring, planned to devastate her with the truth. The Grays had miscalculated with their booby-trapped prize. Nothing could phase Joan anymore, especially after four years of medical school. She accepted the ring as a lost item of a deceased friend. Knowing that the power of the red ring was in good hands now, she flowed backwards out of the portal without moving her feet. Avoiding further reflection, Joan quickly left the room and the energetic template.

Later in the evening, Larry arrived home from a late night at work. Joan met him in the living room just as he placed a light green, Fluorite crystal skull on the coffee table. Joan eyed the object with curious respect before she planted a soft kiss on his cheek.

"Reminds me of something I saw in anatomy lab," Joan told him. "It is too pretty for cadaver lab."

Larry laughed. "It is gorgeous on a light table. The light reflects out of its eyes like two laser beams."

Over cups of hot chocolate and chai, Joan related her experience with the red ring in the portal. "Some of it was skullduggery, though I think that it was worth the effort. I retrieved some information as well as finished the cleanup job. The red ring has something to do with an extraterrestrial gridding system, an old one. Whatever gridding system that included Stonehenge no longer exists. There is only the little bit of gridding that we have been doing on the North American continent." Joan paused briefly as she stared at the crystal skull. "I think there is a connection between your crystal skull and the red ring."

"The red ring belonging to the Regulus star system tracks the crystal skulls," Larry surmised. "It brought Flora to you. There is a replica of Stonehenge in eastern Washington overlooking the Columbia River. That one is one that is now energetically active."

"Wonderful. Let's grid to the Washington Stonehenge." Then Joan asked, changing the subject, "Is that the name of the crystal skull? Some classmates and I named our cadavers when we studied Gross Anatomy."

"Yes, according to those who work with the crystal skulls, it is best to name them before using them in meditation," Larry suggested. "This skull is made of Fluorite, so I called her Flora. It is another connection between the plant and mineral kingdom. Now it is up to us animals to complete the connection---vegetable, mineral, and animal."

The home phone rang and Joan answered it.

"You have perfect timing," Joan told Donna. "I received a red ring in one of the energetic templates and Larry reeled in a crystal skull."

"Great, I'll bring in some world maps and we can do some gridding." Then Donna added, "You wear a red ring."

Joan answered, "Before I had a wedding band, I wore it to deter people away from my personal life. It kept them guessing. I just wear the wedding band on the other hand."

"It still keeps them guessing," Larry joshed, before Joan nudged him back into silence.

"Donna is coming over with world maps," she told him after she hung up. "I have the red ring in my mind's eye. I think I can find the placement of the other crystal skulls on the continents."

A half hour later, Donna walked into the kitchen and spread several copies of a world map on the counter. Larry arranged the maps in front of Joan, who had retrieved her ruby ring from the jewelry box in the bedroom. Several small diamonds offset the small ruby ring, which differed from the one obtained in the portal. She studied the maps carefully with Flora in mind.

"Looking at the North American continent from our bird's eye perspective, we have these points. One point is Unity, Maine because it is connected to several significant world portals. Another point is in Utopia, Texas, which is another theme that we have been energetically gridding. The third point is Mt. Adams, Washington. I am convinced that there is a crystal skull at the base of that remote volcano."

"Adam refers to the first human male form," Donna observed. "Connecting the points makes a triangle, sorta like home plate on a baseball diamond."

"Drop Adam. It is time for a new man to bat at the plate," interrupted Larry. "On the South American continent, we have three points also. Explorers have found buried crystal skulls that have been there for hundreds of thousands of years. One point is on Easter Island. No surprise there. A second point is in the northern Andes with an indigenous tribe called the Mamas. Eight months ago they came out with statements on earth changes and the need to respect Mama Earth or Pachamama. They consider Cocamama as the daughter of Pachamama. Many of the sacred rituals of this secret civilization involve cocoa, which is used to make chocolate."

"I know a few chocolate worshippers in this country," Donna interjected. "They might call it a religion."

"The type of phenylalanines in chocolate are the same found in breast milk," Joan commented. "We use it to treat mild depression without the calories. The human body uses this amino acid to make others like serotonin."

When she finished the explanation, Larry announced the next point. "There is a third location in the Amazon, where a tribe of single-breasted female warriors flourished."

"It is beginning to look almost biological," Donna commented as Joan formed the yin triangle to matched the yang triangle in the northern hemisphere. "By the way, Carrie called just before I left the office. She and Jasper are on their way over. This is really far out stuff."

"Well, they are physicists. They put people on the moon with nothing more than a mathematical equation," Joan remarked. "This should be in their ballpark, especially after the latest sting operation. They captured those who had tortured Carrie during the time wrinkle and busted a Green's base underneath Washington D.C.."

"Green?" Larry questioned.

"The Greens are derivatives of the Grays," Joan answered. They are related to the Green Party and satanic child abuse at the San Francisco Presidio. When unmasked, this alien group is really not for the earth at all. This should take the heat off of Carrie, though she still has the Russian underground and *nada*s harassing her."

Carried ignored Joan's words as she entered the room. She focused on the immediate topic. Bitting her lip, Joan softly hugged Carrie with one arm while the woman leaned over the table to check the map.

"Ruby is the birth stone for Leo, which is the constellation that contains Regulus," Carrie remarked, when she entered the kitchen through the backdoor. "We saw everyone congregated over the kitchen counter through the window. So Jasper suggested that we go around to the kitchen. Donna already told me about the red ring and world grid lines."

Everyone at the counter looked up as they heard her words. Jasper sauntered over to the other side to peer at the world maps. His eyes grew wide and he smiled at the placement of the triangles.

"There is a Spirit Cave in Tibet where the Russians have recorded frequencies coming from the cave," Jasper commented. "It sings whenever a major earthquake is imminent. Only the Tibetian monks know the exact location. Not only does the Singing Cave serve as an alarm system, but it sustains the planet with the emissions."

"Then there is a place in India in the Narmada River where a meteorite impregnated the river bed millions of years ago," Carrie added, studying the world maps by Jasper's side. "The Shiva Lingam is the sacred stone from the river. The stone is a phallic symbol, representing masculine creative energy. Other markings on the stone belong to Yoni, the creative energy of the female."

"Sounds like a scene in *Indiana Jones and the Temple of Doom*," Larry commented.

"It's our first point on the triangle for that part of the world," continued Joan as she penciled in the location. "Thanks," she said to Jasper and Carrie.

"The region by the Narmada River is known for its Maheshwari saris, which is the garment worn by Indian women since the time of the Indus Valley civilization," Jasper continued. "The creative female energy of the saris is very powerful. I traveled there with some friends after college. The natives insist that the Narmada River could change the lifestyle of humans with the power of ecology. Now I wonder whether it serves as metaphysical metaphor rather than a political statement."

"The next point is at Mount Elgon in Kenya, where the world's top marathoners train," Joan commented as she drew a line to the next point. "The final point for the triangle is in Congo, the site of the former

Kongo dia Nlaza. Yanni told me once that he had planted several small crystals skulls in western Africa. This location bears out."

"The Northern triangle of the pair contains a point where I found the dragon egg," Larry said leaning further over the counter. "There's another one at Loch Ness. Nessie guards that site."

"A third point is Lake Hovsgol in Mongolia," Donna observed. "The name translates to 'ocean mother,' which matches our Mama-Earth theme."

"There, we've gridded the planet for its rebirth," Joan announced as she reviewed the world map.

"There's one other detail," Donna added. "The grid includes a utopic theme centered on the mythical sites of Shambala and Belovodia. The long tips of the Eurasia triangle pair point to these regions. The American triangle pair brings this theme forward in a protective inverse or 69 arrangement."

"Many of the points of the triangles lie on major geophysical features such as faults and volcanoes," Larry observed. Loch Ness is on the Glen Fault. Mount Elgon is the caldera of an extinct volcano, whereas Mount Adams is an active volcano in the New World. This grid has been around since the Regulus star civilization."

"The locations of the crystal skulls served as navigation devices for the star sphere containing the Wise Kings. They resemble the conduction wires above an electrical train," Jasper commented. "What is Belovodia?"

"It is the Russian equivalent of Shambala," Carrie told him. "A few years ago, archeologists uncovered a mummy from the Altai Mountains. The melting ice exposed the mummy. There found Scythian tattoos on the body that relate to a shaman sect in the area. This sect is known for their ability to work with time in multiple dimensions."

"Eli says that this served as JFK's connection at Budapest border," Donna interjected. "His naval intelligence work encompassed this group that could work with time. The intelligence operations dubbed them valentines. Remember, we were allies with the Russians in WWII. In England, he watched Profumo/Dion Fortune's esoteric group, which countered Nazi occultism with Lucifer's agenda. Unfortunately, Serpentines infiltrated the group and Carrie paid the price in the time wrinkle."

Joan glanced at Carrie from her map. "Do you think Belovodia knew about time wrinkles? I read about the discovery in *Entering the Circle*, the book written by a Russian psychiatrist. She worked to retrieve the Russian soul. The tattoos images offer some protection."

"Probably," Carrie said. "It is all old stuff. The red ring associated with the portal possibly belonged to the female leader of the Regulus star base. When the Grays raped the star base, they stopped the maturation of the dragon eggs and ended that earthly civilization, which the Pleiades supported. This gridding represents two star lines. Both were destroyed before the Dark Ages. Only the myths exist, supported by secret native cultures."

"And a few astrophysicists," Jasper added as he hugged Carrie with one arm.

"I knew that I could count on you two." Joan nodded with a smile.

"One more thing," Larry said as he hurriedly constructed a map of Gondwanaland. He scribbled on a piece of clean paper left on the counter. After he drew the collection of Antarctica, India, Africa, South America, Australia, and Arabia in one giant landmass, he drew an eye over the locations of the known crystal skull sites.

"This eye reflects the eye in the sky," Donna observed after studying Larry's drawing.

"Not bad for a supercontinent during the time of the early Jurassic," Larry acknowledged. "Like the Nazar eye, it is a protective shield as well as a political statement. Gondwanaland kept a watchful eye on the universe."

"Time for the unveiling," Larry remarked. "Perhaps that is the mystery of the Mayan calendar and the passing of Nibiru in 2012."

Joan stopped suddenly. "There is a very intricately ordered, joyous, and loving world depicted on these maps. The eye is awakening."

Carrie quipped, "According to a book called *Elegant Universe*, there is a fundamental string somewhere."

Convinced, Joan smiled her agreement, "There's a new world dawning."

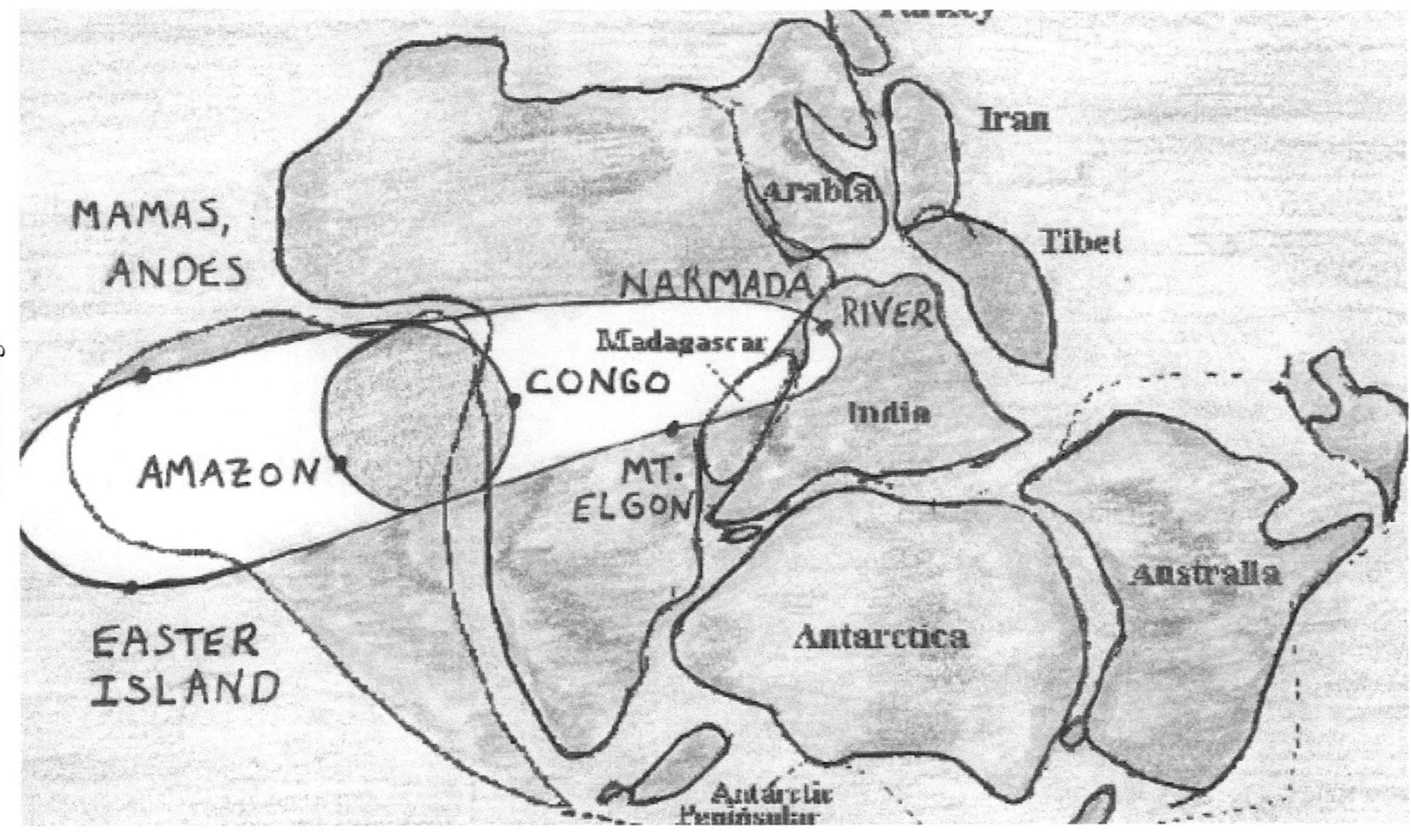

MAMAS, ANDES
Turkey
Iran
Arabia
Tibet
NARMADA
RIVER
Madagascar
CONGO
India
AMAZON
MT. ELGON
Australia
EASTER ISLAND
Antarctica
Antarctic Peninsular

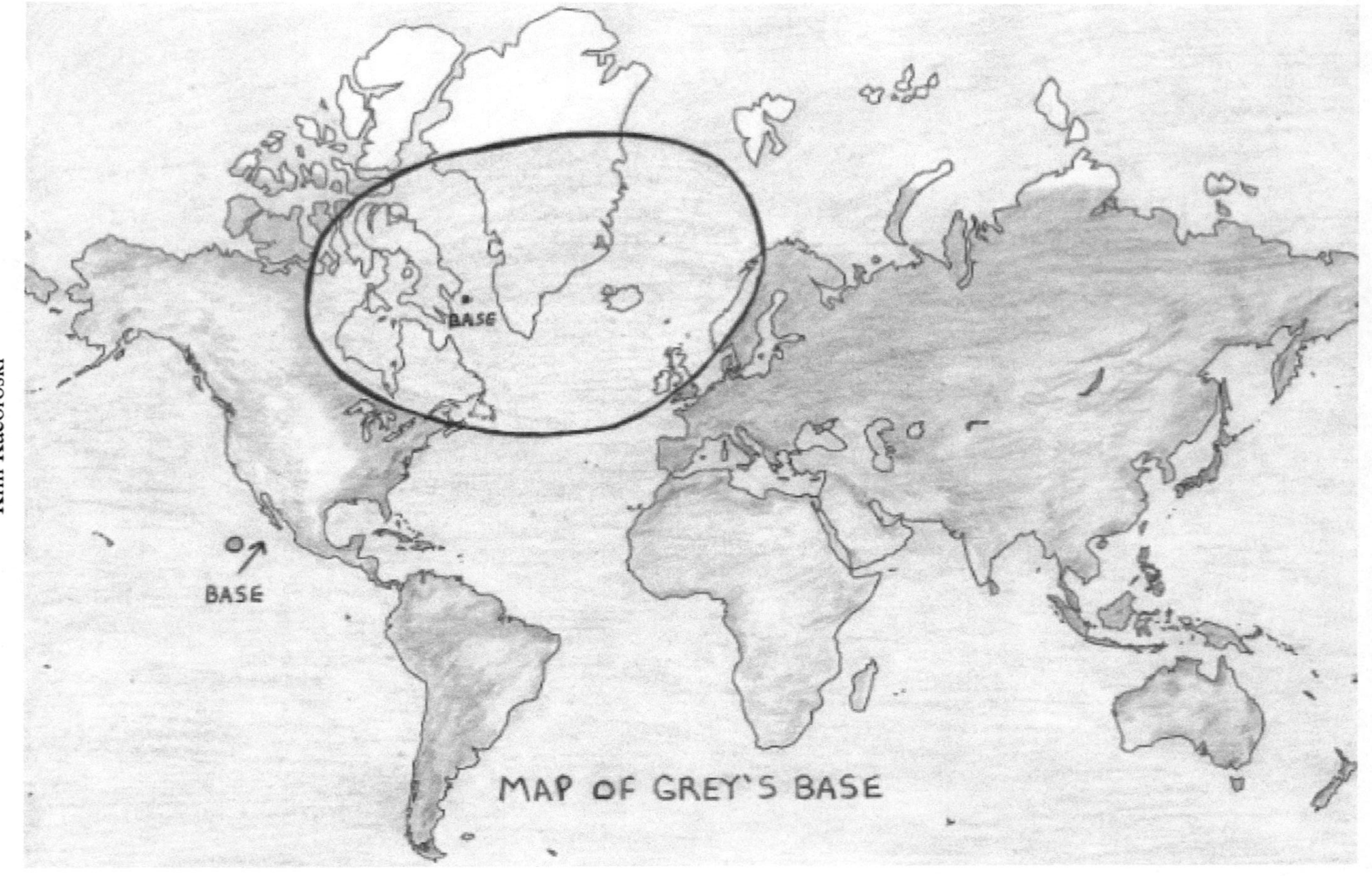
BASE
BASE
MAP OF GREY'S BASE

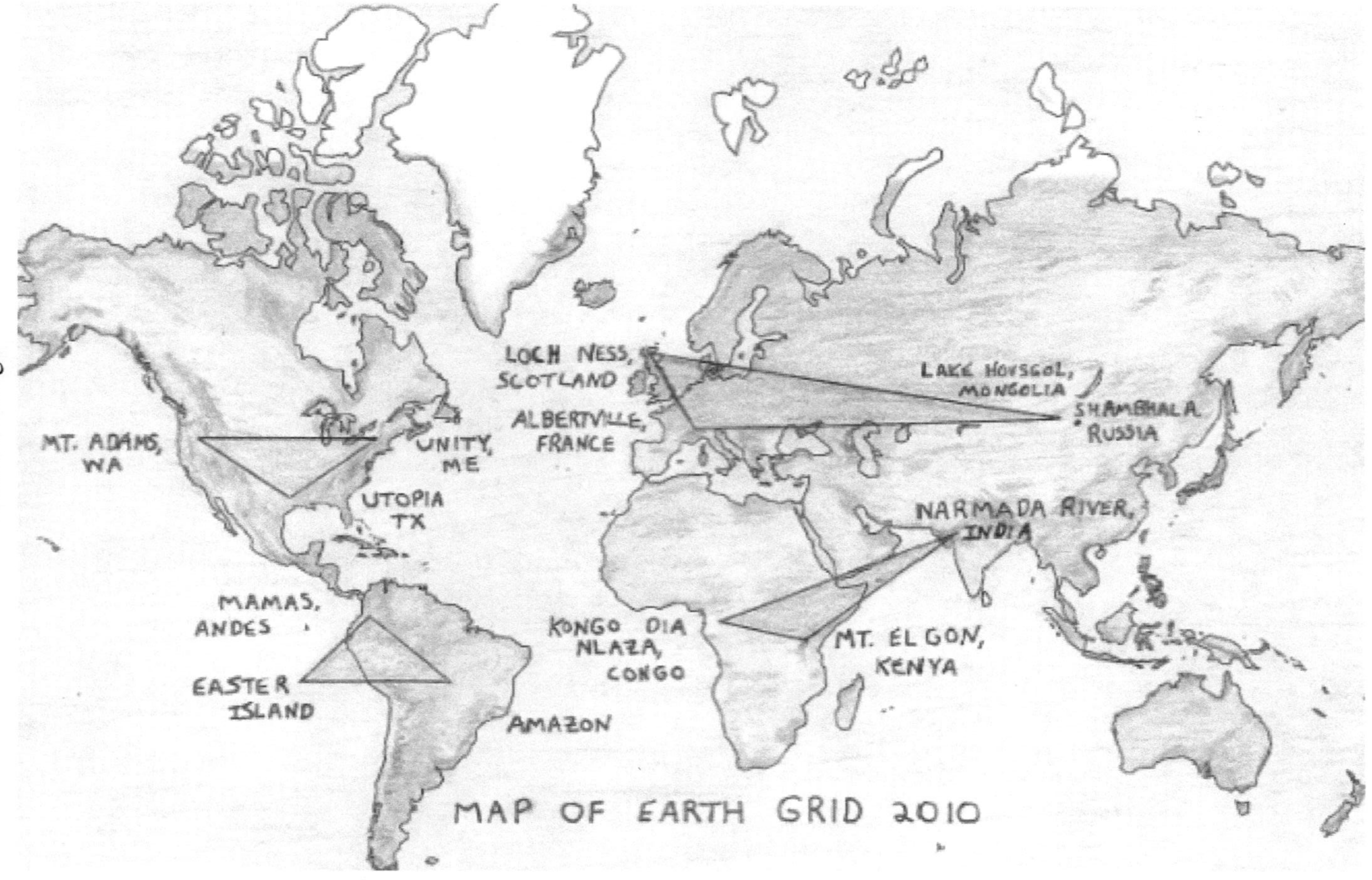
MT. ADAMS, WA
UNITY, ME
UTOPIA TX
LOCH NESS, SCOTLAND
ALBERTVILLE, FRANCE
LAKE HOVSGOL, MONGOLIA
SHAMBHALA, RUSSIA
NARMADA RIVER, INDIA
MAMAS, ANDES
EASTER ISLAND
KONGO DIA NLAZA, CONGO
AMAZON
MT. ELGON, KENYA
MAP OF EARTH GRID 2010